S0-EAQ-584

CANDLELIGHT
Ecstasy Supreme

"YOU'RE A WHAT?" REESE SAID,
HIS FACE DARKENING WITH ANGER.

"I work for an investigation firm in Atlanta. I'm a private eye," Tohni explained softly. "I've reported on you every day for the past two weeks."

"You deceitful little witch! What a fool I've been. Will you make a report on last night, detailing how many times we made love?"

"I know what you're thinking, Reese, but last night I could only think of losing you. And I didn't want that to happen."

"Like hell! You didn't want me out of your sight. What better way to keep an eye on me than to spend the night with me?"

"That's not so," she protested. "I knew that last night would be our last for a while and I just lost—"

"Correction, *honey*. That was our first and last time ever!"

CANDLELIGHT ECSTASY SUPREMES

PARTNERS IN PERIL

Tate McKenna

A CANDLELIGHT ECSTASY SUPREME

Published by
Dell Publishing Co., Inc.
1 Dag Hammarskjold Plaza
New York, New York 10017

Copyright © 1986 by Mary Tate Engels

All rights reserved. No part of this book may be reproduced
or transmitted in any form or by any means, electronic or
mechanical, including photocopying, recording or by any
information storage and retrieval system, without the written
permission of the Publisher, except where permitted by law.

Dell® TM 681510, Dell Publishing Co., Inc.

Candlelight Ecstasy Supreme is a trademark
of Dell Publishing Co.,Inc.

Candlelight Ecstasy Romance®,1,203,540, is a registered
trademark of Dell Publishing Co., Inc., New York, New York

ISBN: 0-440-16804-X

Printed in the United States of America

First printing—February 1986

For Rog, my partner in all things, with love

To Our Readers:

We are pleased and excited by your overwhelmingly positive response to our Candlelight Ecstasy Supremes. Unlike all the other series, the Supremes are filled with more passion, adventure, and intrigue, and are obviously the stories you like best.

In months to come we will continue to publish books by many of your favorite authors, as well as the very finest work from new authors of romantic fiction. As always, we are striving to present unique, absorbing love stories—the very best love has to offer.

Breathtaking and unforgettable, Ecstasy Supremes follow in the great romantic tradition you've come to expect *only* from Candlelight Ecstasy.

Your suggestions and comments are always welcome. Please let us hear from you.

Sincerely,

The Editors
Candlelight Romances
1 Dag Hammarskjold Plaza
New York, New York 10017

PROLOGUE

"Where is Reese Kreuger?"

"We aren't exactly sure, Cornell, but it's just a matter of time."

"And what—exactly—does that mean, Jacoby? My orders were to find him and bring him here. Immediately! This thing has been dragging on for weeks."

"Well, we don't know where he is right now, but it won't be long before we find him," Jacoby said, rushing to reassure his hotheaded boss. "Harrison's working on it. We've checked at Kreuger's apartment several times and haven't been able to catch him there."

"Has he moved?"

"No. We don't think so."

"Then where the hell's he living?"

Jacoby cleared his throat. "It's possible he isn't even in Atlanta right now. We're still checking on it."

"Checking?" Cornell Ansel's dark eyes narrowed. "Where is he? Back in Miami? Or maybe off to the French Riviera? Or is he camped on the EPA's doorstep in Birmingham?"

"Now simmer down, Cornell," Jacoby soothed. "We'll find him."

"Before he squeals?"

"Sure, sure. Harrison is in charge of it, and I know he'll—"

Ansel waved a hand impatiently. "Is Harrison in the outer office?"

Jacoby nodded. "He was on his way. Should be here by now."

Ansel punched one of the numerous buttons alongside his phone. "Dorothy, send Harrison in." He glared at Jacoby, who shuffled from one shiny wing-tip shoe to the other. "I want both of you involved in this. Maybe between the two of you, we can catch this weasel."

Harrison entered the walnut-paneled office. His black pin-striped suit was pressed to perfection, matching the attire of the other two men in the room. But in his eyes was the look of a man about to face a firing squad, for he'd worked with Cornell Ansel long enough to know that the man meant what he said. The directive had been issued weeks ago: Find Reese Kreuger. Unfortunately, they hadn't been able to produce Kreuger; they had no idea where he was.

Harrison halted next to Jacoby and clasped his hands behind his back.

"You wanted to see me, sir?"

Ansel rose from behind his wide desk and paced before the floor-to-ceiling windows

12

overlooking Peachtree Street. The metropolis of Atlanta sprawled in all directions, to the Confederate soldiers carved on Stone Mountain and beyond. In Cornell Ansel's mind, it was *his* city. It had taken him twenty years, but he'd made Atlanta the center of his corporate empire. That empire stretched to New York, Tennessee, Alabama, Mississippi, Texas, Montana, and soon it would extend to Oregon. And he would not let it be destroyed by one man— one man who knew too much.

"What do you really know about Reese Kreuger?" Ansel began.

The two men opposite him exchanged uneasy glances, then Jacoby spoke. "Oh, come on, Cornell. We worked with him for three years. He's a bright guy who knows his chemicals, and basically was a good VP." Jacoby hesitated.

"Is that it?"

"Well, no, sir," Harrison added. "He comes from a wealthy family in Miami, is a chemistry whiz, did a short stint in Vietnam, then married your daughter four years ago. They divorced a year ago, about the time he left the company. Incidentally, he isn't at his family's home in Miami."

"How do you know that? Did you stake it out?"

"Well, no, sir, we called."

Ansel's voice exploded. "You *called?* Didn't it occur to you that he might even be living at his family's home and someone just lied and told you he wasn't there?" Ansel stormed

13

around the room, revealing a festering anger fueled by fear. And he hated the feeling. He hated the fact that that SOB Kreuger could instill such fear in him. Damn the man anyway! He forced his voice into a tight, controlled tone. "Now, gentlemen, let *me* tell you about Reese Kreuger. And I don't want a word of this to go beyond this room. Do you understand?"

Both men affirmed it readily.

"Reese Kreuger is brilliant. He's too damned brilliant for his own good. He isn't right for this corporation, or for any corporation. He has proved he isn't cut out for working for the government. They got rid of him when he started making waves. You know why? He's too damned honest! He can't turn his head when he ought to and can't stay out of matters that don't concern him. And, this time, he's stuck his nose out too far."

"Is he still making threats about compliance?" Jacoby asked.

"It's gone further than threats, Jacoby. I just got a call from someone at the EPA district office in Birmingham. Guess who just called them?" Ansel stopped long enough to adjust the finely crafted vertical blinds so the sun wouldn't glare into the room. The pause provided precisely the emphasis he wanted.

His next two words were like pistol shots. *"Reese Kreuger."*

He paused again to let the words sink in. "He wants to set up a meeting with Michael O'Hara, the district manager. Wants to get

14

some things off his chest. But the boy is smart. Not smart enough to stay married to my Gloria or to keep his mouth shut about us. But smart nonetheless. He hasn't named names yet. *Yet!* Fortunately, they didn't have time to see him right now. O'Hara is out of the office for a few weeks. That gives us time to act. I don't want Kreuger to make it to that meeting. It's crucial that we stop him. Do you understand?"

Jacoby nodded briskly. "I understand, Cornell. Did your connection say where the call came from?"

"No. Only that Kreuger left his name and wanted to set up an appointment for next week. He's supposed to call later and set up a time. That gives us time to find him—and stop him.

"Now I want to give you gentlemen some incentive in this situation. In the next few months we have a chance to get a big contract from the government, involving business in Oregon. It's very important to me to get this contract. Important to all of us.

"However, if Kreuger spills his guts and our name gets smeared, our chances for this contract will be ruined. If Kreuger has his way, our whole operation will be shut down. That means your jobs, gentlemen. I don't want that to happen, and I'm sure you don't either. I want this man silenced."

"Sir, it seems to me that we've already exhausted all our means of finding him," Harrison said. "How do you feel about hiring a private detective?"

Ansel eyed them squarely. "Whatever it takes, Harrison. Just get him. I'm through playing games with Kreuger. It's time to play hardball. I'm ready to negotiate with him. Do you know what I mean?"

"Yessir!" Jacoby and Harrison exchanged glances. They'd discussed the possibility of bringing in professional help and now had the okay to do it. They almost fell over themselves in relief as they retreated from the walnut-paneled office.

CHAPTER ONE

Tohni York stood on tiptoe on the toilet seat in the employees' rest room and peered through the narrow grating near the ceiling. It gave her a sweeping view of the restaurant's parking lot near the tip of a silvery lake. *And of Reese Kreuger.*

There he was, right on time. Easiest and most enjoyable "bulldogging" she'd ever done in all her years at Eagle Eye Investigations. Usually it was boring as hell to hide and watch someone. Often the most exciting part was scouting out a remote phone booth from which to call the report into the office. Well, that was no problem here. The whole town was remote.

But this guy was different. The fact that he was easy on the eyes might have had something to do with her enjoying this assignment. But that was it, because Tohni knew this was strictly business.

"Mandy?" A heavy knock on the rest-room door interrupted Tohni's thoughts. "You gonna take all night? We've got a roomful of hungry piranhas out here! The boss is yelling."

"Be right there, Betty June." Tohni hopped down from her lookout, assured that Reese Kreuger was on his way.

She stood before the mirror and adjusted the tiny cap that was perched like a lace doily on top of her short black curls. If I had a fuller figure, she mused, I'd look like an eighteenth-century barroom wench. Instead I look like a little girl dressed up in Great-aunt Fanny's clothes. She smiled to herself. In a way, that's exactly what she was doing—dressing up and pretending. What a wonderful job! She loved it, especially the cloak-and-dagger part of it. She thrived on the thrill of the chase and took pride in her creative disguises. Some of her colleagues even came to her for quick make-overs.

She tugged at the short tight skirt, fluffed her apron, and smoothed the vest that was laced up the middle and was supposed to emphasize a tiny waist and full bosom. On her, it emphasized how tiny she was all over. With a sigh she reminded herself that there were times when being five feet two came in handy.

Adjusting the nametag above her left breast, she opened the rest-room door. With that simple act she became Mandy Johnson, the most flirtatious waitress at the Catfish King. The subject of her surveillance, Reese Kreuger, ate there every night, since it was the only decent restaurant within ten miles of Chickamauga Lake in Tennessee. And she always managed to wait on his table.

18

Tohni halted beside the shelf of prepared food that extended from the kitchen. With the skill of a Chinese juggler, she balanced four plates piled high with fried catfish, cole slaw, and hush puppies and proceeded across the crowded room. She flashed a welcoming smile at Reese, who stood patiently waiting to be seated.

He always asked for the small table near the big windows overlooking a portion of the glistening Chickamauga Lake. She wondered if he liked to sit there because he appreciated the magnificent view of the lake or because he knew it was her area. Or maybe he sat there because it was the best spot from which to watch the restaurant's clients come and go. After all, he was on the lam.

She saw the hostess leading him to his usual table.

"Be with you in a minute," she promised as she whizzed past him, balancing two trays with glasses of water and mugs of tea and coffee.

When she returned to his table, Tohni smiled warmly. She smacked her gum and drawled breathlessly, "How've you been, honey?"

"Just fine, Mandy. And you?" His voice was mellow, as if he'd had voice lessons or had at one time been a disc jockey. She knew better though. He was a poor little rich kid from Connecticut whose parents had retired to Miami Beach. He'd been around the world pursuing his interests, mainly women, until a few years ago.

19

After a short stint in the army, he had seemed to settle down, marrying a wealthy Atlanta socialite and going to work for her father. Now, though, his life had fallen apart. Reese had skipped town, and his former employer was looking for him. Tohni wouldn't spare any sympathy for him. Interest, maybe. But not sympathy.

"How am I?" She sighed and rolled her gray eyes comically. "I can't please anybody tonight. Bring more fish to this table. Slaw's too salty over there. Hush puppies need to be returned and cooked longer. Sometimes this place drives me crazy."

He shrugged and glanced around. "Oh, I don't know. You seem to have things under control."

"Honey, if there's one thing I'm good at, it's control," she sassed confidently. "By this time of night things usually calm down. But tonight everybody wants the special. Fried catfish. You want it too, sport?" She snapped her gum and tugged on a dark curl.

"Sure. Why not? Do you recommend it?"

"What I recommend isn't on the menu," she murmured with a teasing grin.

"And what's that, Mandy?" He gave her an innocent look and folded his arms across the menu. She noticed how tanned his hands were, and that he wasn't wearing any rings. He'd removed them long ago, for there weren't any white lines either. It was her job to be observant.

Her eyes snapped back to his. "Candlelight, soft music, and rainbow trout, broiled with garlic butter and slivered almonds."

"Hmm, sounds like trout amandine. Do you serve it here?"

She shrugged. "Whatever you call it, we don't have it. Now as for the soft music, you won't find that here either. But I have a stereo at home that picks up Chattanooga stations just fine. And I always have a few candles on hand."

"Is that an invitation, Mandy?"

Her gray eyes grew large. She tossed her raven curls and drawled prettily, "Why, honey, you know I'm not allowed to fraternize with the customers."

"I see," he mused, laughter dancing in his beautiful blue eyes. "But nobody said anything about flirting, huh?"

She winked. "A little flirting never hurt anybody, I always say. You made up your mind about your order?"

"Well," he said, pondering, letting his eyes travel reluctantly back to the menu. "If you don't have trout amandine, I'll settle for the fried catfish special."

"Listen, sport, my mama always told me not to settle for less. That goes for life as well as for fishing."

"Life as well as fishing, huh?" He laughed.

"Gotta keep my customers happy. And smiling. Did you know you have a darling smile with that cute little dimple?" She glanced up and noticed her boss glaring at her from the

21

kitchen. It wouldn't do to get fired, since she was just building a rapport with Mr. Kreuger. "My boss is giving me the eye, so I'd better cut this short. What do you want to drink with your catfish? Beer's best with fried fish. We have some very mild draft."

"Okay, make it a draft."

She flashed him another smile as she took the menu and sashayed away.

Reese had practically finished his catfish platter when Tohni finally found time to stop and chat again. "Hey, honey, you doing all right? Can I get you another beer?" She took his plate and half-empty beer into account, then smiled to herself. Maybe she was getting the hang of this waitressing after all.

"No thanks, Mandy. I'm fine."

"Well, how was the catfish?"

"Very good. But you were right about the trout and soft music. Sounds better to me than this."

"I'll tell the boss." She grinned, snapping her gum. "Maybe next week's special will be . . . what did you call it? Trout—"

"Amandine."

"Yeah. Trout amandine. Sounds snazzy. Like you, sport. I'll bet you're a snazzy man. Used to fancy food and all."

He smiled slightly and the dimple showed in his right cheek. "I've been around a little."

"I'll bet you've been around a lot. Where're you from?"

"Atlanta."

22

"Just up here to do a little fishing?"

"That's right. And to catch up on some work."

"Is that what you keep reading every night when you eat? Your work? Boy, your boss must be a real stickler if you can't even take a vacation without doing some work. I'd hate that." She paused and sighed. "You're always so serious. But I *like* a serious man."

He shrugged. "Not much going on around here for entertainment. Actually, reading gives me something to do while I'm eating alone."

"You know something, sport? You remind me of a little statue my high-school English teacher had sitting on her desk. It was of this real good-looking man with lots of muscles, you know? If I remember correctly, he was nude." She narrowed her twinkling eyes. "Anyway, he sat with his chin in his hand like you do when you're reading. Only he was just thinking. That's what Mrs. Pierce called him. The thinker."

"Of course." Reese nodded. "There's a statue by Rodin called *The Thinker*. But, Mandy, I'd hardly put myself in that category."

She shrugged happily. "But I would. Is that what you are, honey? A thinker? I *like* a man who thinks."

He suppressed a grin. "I suppose so."

"Well, I know one thing." Tohni rolled her eyes and poked her pencil behind one ear. "My mama used to say, 'All work and no play makes

Jack a dull boy.' You need to loosen up and have some fun."

He crooked one eyebrow. "This place is hardly jumping with nightlife, Mandy."

"What's your name, honey?" she asked, shifting one slender hip into prominence. She watched his eyes travel up her shapely thigh.

Caught off-guard, he said automatically, "Reese Kreuger."

"Well, Reese honey, my philosophy is, Fun is anywhere two people want to make it happen."

"That so? Well, Mandy, are you offering to show me where to have fun around here?"

Before she could answer, a male voice called across the dining room. "Where's my favorite gal? Hey, Mandy! What're you doin' flirtin' with somebody else? I thought you were mine!"

She looked up and winked and waved at someone all the way across the room. "Hiya, Virgil! Be right with you!" Turning back to Reese, she promised, "Maybe someday, honey. But not tonight. I have to work late."

She flounced away, fully aware that Reese Kreuger's eyes followed her across the room. What she didn't realize was that every man's eyes in the place observed her sweeping movement, with unanimous masculine approval.

"Hi, Virg! What can I get for you? Catfish special?" Tohni stood with her pencil poised, but her mind was racing with the valuable information she'd just gained from her subject.

He'd admitted what she suspected. Reese Kreuger from Atlanta. Now if she could just wrap this up before she had to follow through with showing him where to have a "good time!"

The next morning dawned gray and gloomy, and Tohni was so tempted to stay in bed. She snuggled down under the blanket and listened to the rain pelt the roof of the small cabin she was renting. *Reese Kreuger, why do you have to jog so damned early in the morning?*

It struck her that he might be doing just what she was this morning. Snuggling. But she knew better. He was so damned disciplined. He was probably warming up with jumping jacks at this very moment. Begrudgingly, she rolled out of her warm refuge and put on hot water for instant coffee.

Half an hour later she was hidden in the branches of a hickory tree, binoculars focused on the lean, muscular figure of Reese Kreuger as he jogged his usual two miles. She shivered and hoped he would hurry. From her lofty perch Tohni could follow him along the tree-lined Lakeside Road, around the north edge of the lake, down the deep ravine where there were no cabins because of frequent flooding, and back to Lakeside Road.

Tohni took a deep breath full of the damp smells around her. Green hickory nuts, un-raked leaves, new sprigs. A dogwood tree across the road was starting to bloom, a surefire herald of spring in the South. She wondered if Reese Kreuger paid attention to these things. Probably not. He was too busy *thinking.*

Focusing on him again, she could see he was on the back loop, heading home. Actually, he couldn't have picked a lovelier spot in which to hide out than the wooded area around Chickamauga Lake in eastern Tennessee. This had been one stakeout she'd thoroughly enjoyed. Kreuger had been relatively easy to find, and watching him had been pure pleasure.

A movement through the trees caught her eye and Tohni spotted Kreuger at the top of the hill, heading for the home stretch. And her. She braced her feet against two branches and held her breath. It wouldn't do for her to come clambering out of the tree at this moment. She could just imagine the look on his face!

His official facts and stats, as listed in his file were: Reese Kreuger, divorced once, presently unmarried; 33 years old, 5'11", 170 lbs., light brown hair, blue eyes. Distinguishing marks: single crease, right cheek; no scars.

Through a woman's eyes, though, Tohni saw Reese Kreuger as a handsome male with not an ounce of flab on him. Her personal stats read: tawny blond hair, daring blue eyes, a darling dimple in his right cheek, and a perfectly bronzed body that she'd like to check over thoroughly for scars.

Yes, she'd judged him a ten. Plus a few points for being so intelligent. *A thinker.*

Still, Kreuger was in dutch with his former

boss and ex–father-in-law, Cornell Ansel, who headed a large toxic-waste disposal company. She couldn't help speculating on what the trouble with Kreuger might be. Maybe he's late on alimony payments to Ansel's beautiful daughter, Gloria. Could it be that he'd swiped some trade secrets from Ansel Chemical Corporation and the big daddy was angry? Perhaps Kreuger had been holding out for more money on a big deal with Ansel. All she'd been told was that they wanted him because they were ready to negotiate.

Reese Kreuger jogged past Tohni's hickory tree. She could hear him panting, almost feel the heat radiating from his body as he turned into the driveway of his cabin. His T-shirt was soaked with the drizzling rain and clung to his torso, outlining the broad shoulders and trim waist. In fact, he was soaked all the way down to his running shoes. Nice buns, Reese Kreuger, and nice legs, she thought as he disappeared into his cabin.

Tohni poked quarters into the pay phone outside a 7-Eleven store until the connection was made. "Joe? I'm pretty sure I've found him. We're in a sleepy little community near Chickamauga Lake, north of Chattanooga."

"Great. Make a positive ID as soon as you can, Tohni, and keep a tail on him. Report all movement."

"Sure thing, Joe. I think I can nail him down within a couple of days."

"Tohni, for Pete's sake, don't lose him. Don't let that man out of your sight."

"My pleasure, Joe."

CHAPTER TWO

"Barbecue's the special tonight, Reese. That is your name, isn't it, honey?" Tohni angled her head flirtatiously toward Reese and felt that darned doily shift on her head.

"That's me," he acknowledged as he studied the menu. "Are you recommending the barbecue tonight, Mandy?"

"It's pretty good. But I've tasted better. There's a little hole-in-the-wall place in my hometown of Fort Payne that fixes the very best barbecue in the world. They also have some of the finest sorghum you've ever had. Not that syrupy stuff either. It's the real McCoy. Nice and thick."

"The real McCoy, eh?" Reese leaned back and smiled, obviously enjoying her folksy chatter. "So you're from Alabama, Mandy?"

"Yep." She nodded with a wink. "Can't you tell from my accent? Folks around here know exactly where I'm from the minute I open my mouth." She smiled broadly.

Joe would die laughing if he could see her now. And hear her! But her mother would be embarrassed to tears. Tohni could imagine her wailing, *My baby, acting like a hussy!* Vera Lee had never been able to understand why Tohni liked working as a private detective anyway. Actually, Tohni thought it was similar to being an actress, especially at times like this when she took on a new identity.

"Your accent is quite . . . pronounced, but I must admit I can't distinguish a Tennessee accent from an Alabama accent. Have you lived up here long?"

"Naw, just got here. Fact is, I just started this job last week. Doing pretty good for a beginner, don't you think?"

"Oh, you're doing fine." He nodded, assessing the very fine way her waitress's uniform fit her shape.

"What about you, Reese? How long have you been up here?"

"A couple of weeks."

"Are you planning to stay long?"

"It depends."

"Depends on whether you get your work done, or if you catch your limit of fish?" she quizzed. As long as he was willing to chat with her, she might as well find out as much as possible directly from the horse's mouth.

"A little of both, I guess," he answered vaguely.

"What are you working so hard on, Reese?" She arched her neck and gazed curiously at the notebook he'd filled with obscure figures.

He made no move to show her his work.

"Just some details on the chemical composition of the lake here."

"This lake? Chickamauga Lake?" She raised her eyebrows, honestly surprised at his answer.

"Yes."

"Now that sounds like something a Thinker would be doing. You don't work for the government, do you, honey?"

"No, Mandy. I don't."

"Then who do you work for?"

He looked steadily at her for a moment, and Tohni thought she detected a degree of turbulence in his deep blue eyes. For sure, they had lost their joy. "I work for various companies. I'm a private consultant."

"Consultant, huh?" She shifted from one foot to the other, letting her skirt creep up a bit of thigh. "Just what do you consult about?"

"Mostly chemical problems. Things like toxic-waste disposal."

She wrinkled her nose. "Disposal? Is that anything like garbage?"

"Yes, you could call it that. Garbage from large industrial companies. Everything has by-products or waste, and much of it is toxic. That means it's dangerous to the environment. And it has to be contained and disposed of properly or it will contaminate everything around it for years to come. It's like dumping poison."

She narrowed her eyes, and sable lashes met at the corners. "Is this what you've been studying here night after night?"

"Afraid so." He nodded.

"How absolutely boring." She sighed heavily. "I thought you were spending all this time studying something really interesting, like how to be a movie star or something."

He chuckled good-naturedly. "It's not exactly titillating, is it?"

"Titillating?" she huffed. "Why, honey, it's as dry as snuff. And twice as ugly. No wonder you don't have a girl friend, Reese. Nobody wants to talk about garbage!" Tohni snapped her gum and shoved a dark curl behind an ear.

He chuckled. "Thanks for the advice, Mandy, but I don't usually discuss toxic waste with my women."

"Oh, really? Well, what do you talk about with your women?"

He pursed his lips and leaned forward with his muscular forearms on the table. "I usually let them take the lead. Then I follow. Take our present conversation, for instance. You were the one who asked about my work, and I just let you pursue it."

"Yes," she admitted with a grin. "But I'm different."

"Oh? How's that?"

She batted her large gray eyes. "I'd listen to you blab on just about anything, honey, simply to see those luscious blue eyes of yours light up. And to watch that cute little dimple dig into your cheek."

He flashed her an embarrassed smile; his white teeth contrasted with his golden skin.

32

"You know all the right things to say to a man, Mandy."

"I notice you aren't wearing a wedding ring, but do you have a girl friend back home?" She pouted slightly.

"No, Mandy. I'm divorced. And no particular girl friend right now."

"Oh, good." She batted her eyes again and smiled grandly. "I'm just curious, Reese. Wouldn't want you leading me on with that gorgeous smile of yours."

"And you? Anyone special, Mandy?"

"Me? No, not me," she murmured shyly. "That's why I moved up here to Tennessee. Back in Fort Payne my boyfriend and I broke up, and I just wanted to get away from him and . . ." At this moment she felt she had Reese Kreuger wrapped right around her little finger.

He nodded understandingly. "Sometimes getting away is the best solution."

"You're right about that," she agreed. "Well, Reese, I have to get to work or I'm going to lose this job too. Did you decide on the barbecue?"

"Looks like I'll have to settle for it, until you can take me down to Fort Payne and we can have the real McCoy."

She grinned and popped her gum excitedly. "It's a deal, honey. I'd love to take the Thinker to God's country for the best barbecue in the world! And I wouldn't mind a bit if my former boyfriend saw us!"

"I think you're trying to use me, Mandy." He laughed cheerfully.

If you only knew, Reese Kreuger, Tohni thought as she sashayed across the room.

Obtaining positive ID of Reese Kreuger was a minor challenge for Tohni. It was one thing for a surveillance subject to admit his name, and yet another to prove his identity for the satisfaction of a client. It took some thinking, but Tohni came up with an idea that just might work.

She checked out her new disguise in the mirror. Fluffing her hair, she decided that the best part of her new look was the blond wig. She always loved the opportunity to be a blonde. And she'd wanted to know all along how Reese responded to blondes. Here was her chance.

On second thought, maybe the best part was the exaggerated bosom she'd given herself, emphasized by the white bib overalls. Now she could see how Reese Kreuger reacted to a buxom female. As if that wasn't enough, she had chosen an eye-catching deep-plum sweater and plum-colored socks to match. She rolled her overalls almost up to her knees so the socks and white tennis shoes would show up nicely. And oh, boy, did they!

Before walking out the door Tohni grabbed her glasses, a most crucial element in her disguise. She started the car and peeped into the rearview mirror at herself. The cat-eyed glasses sparkled brilliantly with the rhinestones outlining their shape, and she laughed fiendishly. She looked like a tacky teenager from the fifties.

It was a shame that only Reese Kreuger would see her in this one!

Tohni proceeded through the necessary steps in case anyone was watching. She drove past Reese's cabin to her first stop, at Ward Sutton's house. Sutton owned the string of lakeside cabins and had rented one to Reese a month ago. She'd discovered that Sutton was an old family friend of the Kreugers' and had given Reese several summer jobs when he was a teenager. As expected, Sutton wasn't home. The next two cabins were empty, but she knocked anyway. Next was Reese Kreuger's cabin. She knew he was home, because she'd watched him all day.

Tohni took a deep breath and knocked, fully expecting Reese to open the door. But when he did, she wasn't prepared for her own powerful reaction. For a full thirty seconds she stared at him, thunderstruck by the sight of him, dressed casually. She'd never before seen him on his own territory, where he worked and relaxed.

His tawny hair was slightly disheveled, his shirt unbuttoned all the way down and hanging loose to reveal a tantalizing mat of chest hair that disappeared down into his skintight jeans. Her traitorous eyes traveled down to see that his feet were bare. He was one sexy man!

She gulped. This was a situation that flirty

Mandy Johnson could handle with aplomb while she snapped her gum and flirted. The real Tohni York would be cool and collected, even though she was steaming on the inside. But this "new" person in white overalls and glitter glasses didn't know what to do.

"H-hi," she stammered. "I'm glad you're home."

If Tohni was speechless, Reese Kreuger was astounded by the purple and white apparition standing before him. He rubbed his hand quickly over his eyes. Maybe he'd been working too long. He blinked again. Nope, there was definitely a blond bombshell in anklets and tennis shoes on his doorstep.

"You are? Why?" he asked.

"Well, I—I'm Donna Dunlap, field rep for Hamilton County Cable TV, and I'm trying to find Mr. Sutton."

"He isn't home."

"Oh, no. It's urgent that I find him."

"Urgent? What's wrong?" Reese moved closer to the open door.

Tohni pulled up straight, trying in vain to make herself taller. But five-two didn't go far in tennis shoes. "His cable TV bill is overdue, and I have to collect it today or it'll be cut off."

Reese leaned forward. "Cable TV? And it's urgent?"

"Oh, definitely," Tohni affirmed with growing fervor for her new role. "You see, he's already late with his payment and today's the

36

last day. If he doesn't pay up, I'm going to have to cut him off. That's part of my job."

"Well, he's gone to Knoxville on business and won't be back for a couple of days."

"That'll be too late."

"Too late for what?"

"Too late to save the cable. I'll just have to cut him off. That means all these cabins will be without color TV. No cartoons for the kids. No soaps for the ladies. No late-night movies for the adults. This weekend they're showing *Casablanca*. Now you don't want them to miss Bogey!"

"People don't come up here to watch TV!" he boomed. "They come up here to fish and get away."

"Maybe you do, but others want to watch cable, Mister, uh, Mister—?"

"Kreuger."

"Even if you don't like to watch TV, Mr. Kreuger, other folks do. And I know for a fact that it's important to Mr. Sutton's business that he keep his cable going."

"If it's that important, why hasn't he paid his bill?"

She shrugged. "I don't know. Maybe he overlooked it. Maybe he didn't have the money."

"Well, we'll get it straightened out when he gets back."

"Like I said, that'll be too late. Even if he decides to keep it, it'll cost him more money."

"How's that?"

She checked off the items on her fingers. "Twenty bucks for re-hookup. Ten for office paperwork for dropping and rehooking him. Service charge, we call it. Then another ten to reconnect the movie channel."

"Oh, good grief!" he grumbled. "Okay, okay, I'll pay it for him."

"That's mighty nice of you, Mr. Kreuger. They're very sticky about this sort of thing at the home office."

"How much is it?"

Tohni hesitated a moment. She had to make it more than the reasonable amount of money he might be carrying in his pocket. Joe said she needed an official document for ID, like a check. "Fifty-eight, twenty-three."

"Fifty-eight bucks? For cable TV?" he exploded.

"Fifty-eight, twenty-three. I told you, he's late paying his bill. Actually, two months late."

"Well, if it's that much, I'll have to write you a check."

Tohni tried not to respond too eagerly. "That'll be fine."

"Will you accept one from an out-of-town bank?"

She gazed up at him and smiled. "Sure. With the proper ID. Your driver's license will do."

"Okay. I'll be right back." When he moved away, Tohni breathed a sigh of relief. At that moment she wasn't sure if she was relieved because he was playing right into her hands, or because his gorgeous golden body was out of her sight. She took a few deep breaths and gave herself a stern warning.

When he returned, she made an elaborate show of writing down his license number and comparing the addresses on his license and the check. She scribbled a receipt and handed it to him. He scrutinized the top of the page, where she'd printed: HAMILTON COUNTY CABLE COMPANY.

"We're a small operation," she explained quickly. "Serving a large area. Well, thank you very much, Mr. Kreuger. I'm sure Mr. Sutton will be ever so grateful to you."

"Yeah, sure," Reese mumbled as he watched the woman in purple and white retreat rapidly to her car.

Tohni smugly tucked the check that identified Reese Kreuger into her bib pocket. She'd accomplished what she'd gone after. Joe would laugh all over the place if he could see her, but he'd also commend her. She could hear him expound, "Well done, kid! Clever idea. I knew I hired you for some good reason." She should feel proud of herself.

So why did she feel like a heel? Like she'd just cheated Reese Kreuger? And herself.

Oh, she hadn't cheated him out of the money, because she'd never cash the check. But she'd cheated him just the same, and she felt awful.

Tohni jerked the car into gear and took off. Damn it! Surely she wasn't letting this man get to her. After all, he was just a job. She couldn't

let herself care about the subjects of her surveillance. By the weekend they might be
wrapping this case up anyway. Then it would
be "Good-bye, Reese Kreuger. I'll never see
you again."

The thought wrenched her stomach. She
didn't want to say "Good-bye, Reese." Didn't
want to think of never seeing the golden-
haired man with the electric-blue eyes again.
Oh, dear God, what was happening to her?
Maybe Mandy Johnson's character was taking
over her life and doing something crazy to her
feelings. But that was ridiculous! Mandy wasn't
a real person!

Tohni flew down the highway to the cabin
she'd rented. Once inside she leaned breathlessly against the door and dug out his check.
With a shaky finger she traced his scrawling
signature. *Reese Kreuger, you're just another
subject,* she repeated over and over again.

But her heart didn't believe it.

Tohni York, alias Mandy Johnson, glanced
around surreptitiously before feeding the pay
phone her quarters. After a pause the connection was complete. "Joe? I have a positive ID. I
have his check in my hand, complete with Atlanta address and phone number. And I've
seen his Georgia driver's license."

"Great job, kid! And quick too. I knew I hired
you for some good reason! Stick with him
now."

"How much longer, Joe?" She didn't think

40

she could hold out much longer. Already she was having trouble sleeping, thinking about this man too much. She just wanted to wind the case up and go home as quickly as possible.

"Hang on to him a few more days, Tohni. Ansel is out of town and nobody wants to act without him. So if they're willing to pay for us to keep tabs on him, just keep playing your game, kid."

She winced at his choice of words. *Playing your game.* It made her feel even more as if she were cheating Reese. "Okay, Joe."

"And, Tohni, for God's sake don't lose him now. Notify me immediately if he makes a move. We'll have to act then for sure."

"Yeah, sure, Joe. I won't lose him." She hung up and leaned her forehead against the phone. *Damn it, Tohni! Get a hold of yourself. You're only playing a game! You've known it all along! Lesson number one: Don't get personally involved!*

Tohni fumbled in her purse and popped a stick of fruit-flavored gum into her mouth. Mandy Johnson was back in charge. Tohni was beginning to hate her. Beginning to hate herself for what she was doing.

CHAPTER THREE

The unkempt old fisherman let his fishing line dangle over the side of the boat and float aimlessly with the current. But catching fish was the furthest thing from the old fisherman's mind as he pulled his frayed straw hat down over his eyes and trained his binoculars on the two figures on shore.

Suddenly, the fishing line tautened and the reel began to whir. The old fisherman stared angrily at the fishing rod, at the sure signs that a fish was on the other end of the line. He dropped his binoculars and grabbed the rod. There was nothing to do but reel in the darned fish.

As he lifted it into the boat he stared at the monster and muttered, "My mama always said, 'When you go fishing, be ready to net a big one!' Now what do I do with you?"

The fish lay in the bottom of the boat, its gills quivering, wheezing for life.

"Hold on there a minute. I'll get you loose. Let me see how this contraption works here." With one toe braced on the fish's head, the old fisherman grimaced and struggled to loosen the shiny hook from the fish's lower lip. Finally, with much effort and many muttered curses, he managed to free it.

Seeming grateful, the large bass flopped around in the bottom of the boat, spraying water everywhere.

"Jumping Jehoshaphat!" muttered the fisherman as he carefully lifted the fish with both hands and threw it over the back side of the boat. He wiped his hands on his pants and dropped his line back into the water. Reseating himself, he pulled the straw hat down over his eyes and fumbled for the discarded binoculars.

Ward Sutton shaded his eyes with his hand, noticing the old fisherman's good luck. "Fish are biting this morning, Reese. Let's get a move on." He lugged a bait box out to the pier where his flat-bottomed fishing boat was tied.

When Ward returned to the grassy shore, Reese was sorting through the rods they would take today. Ward motioned with his head to the old fisherman in the boat. "Danged if he didn't catch another one. Wonder who he is?"

Since there was no answer from Reese, he lapsed into silence, then drifted into reminiscence. "Yeah, it's good to have you around, boy. Reminds me of old times when you were just a squirt and we used to go fishing together. Remember those times, Reese?" The old man's pale blue eyes twinkled with the memories.

Reese leaned back on his haunches and

chuckled. "Yeah, Ward, in those days you were the only one who could handle me."

"I remember the first time your dad sent you down here by yourself." He paused to laugh. "You were all arms and legs, clumsy as a dadburn oaf."

"I was halfway into adolescence and couldn't walk across the room without tripping over myself," Reese added, handing Ward a couple of rods.

"The following year, though, you were a different kid," Ward said with a different tone to his voice. "More serious and damned rebellious."

Reese shook his head. "I remember rebelling against everything my dad said. I appreciate your stabilizing influence on my life during those years, Ward. Without it, I don't know where I'd be today."

"Aw, you would've made it okay, boy. You're too smart to foul it all up completely. But you came away from the war changed again."

Reese started toward the pier. "I guess everybody came back from 'Nam changed, Ward. I didn't see much action, but sure as hell got my eyes opened. I was halfway through med school when I joined up, and they sent me straight to a medical unit. Oh, God, the horror stories I could tell!"

Ward trailed along behind Reese with two creels and some extra tackle. "You got into a little trouble there, didn't you, boy?"

"Only because I told my superior officer

about the dangers of Agent Orange. I explained my chemical background and how I'd studied chemistry for years. I told them the chemicals in Agent Orange were some of the most dangerous ever made, and insisted the spraying be stopped immediately. Hell, I was naive enough to believe they'd listen to me, an upstart college kid! You know what they did? Shipped me out quick with a warning to keep my mouth shut. Like a fool, I complied. Now look at all the trouble they're having over it."

"You're still fighting the establishment, aren't you, Reese?"

"Yeah," Reese admitted, pausing to watch the old fisherman in the boat drag in another fine catch. "Hell, Ward, I guess it's the story of my life. I'm always rebelling against something. Do you think I'm nuts for bucking the big guns this time?"

"You want my honest opinion?" Ward came to a stop and looked out over the water. "I think you're treading on dangerous territory. Ansel is not a man to cross. Get him riled enough and you're going to be in deep trouble."

"Oh, hell, Ward, you're right. I've seen him in action and it is not a pretty sight. Don't forget, he was my father-in-law for three years. Damned harsh man, except when it came to his little Gloria."

Ward shook his head. "Even from the beginning I felt that marriage was doomed. She just wasn't your type, Reese."

45

"I wish I'd realized it before . . . before I got so involved with everything."

"She's not still causing you trouble, is she? After . . . how long has it been now?"

"Nearly two years," Reese said. "Actually, I was lucky to get out of the divorce as cleanly as I did. But Gloria had something to do with that. Even though she liked to play around she had a streak of decency."

Ward cocked his head and grinned. "Now that sounds like a contradiction if I ever heard one."

"Yeah, I guess so," Reese agreed with a derisive chuckle. "Gloria's all right. She's out of my life completely now. It's her old man I can't seem to shake." He stepped down into the boat, and Ward handed him the fishing equipment piece by piece.

"Why don't you steer clear of Ansel? Can't you just let it drop? What's in it for you, Reese?"

"Mostly trouble so far. But, Ward, somebody's got to speak out. Too many people sit back and do nothing. Everyone who knows anything about Ansel Chemical's operations is under Ansel's thumb. Everyone but me."

"But why do you have to be the one to do something?" Ward thrust his fist in the air. "Are you the public's guardian angel?"

Reese chuckled to ease the tension. "Why *not* me? I know what Ansel's doing. Worse yet, I know too much about what these chemicals can do to the environment. And to people. I know the damage that's already been done, and what's happening today. All I want is for somebody, an agency or whatever, to keep it under control. If it's monitored properly, the harm will be minimal. Right now, what they're doing is against the law."

"Then let the law handle it," Ward responded. "You stay out of it."

"I can't, Ward. Don't you understand? I'm the only one who knows and is willing to talk. The law can't act without me and others like me who are willing to blow the whistle. I've let it go unreported so many times in the past, I simply can't let it happen again. First in 'Nam. Then countless times while I worked for the company. Finally I decided I couldn't live with myself if I kept quiet any longer. Ansel's getting away with . . . murder."

Ward's eyes narrowed. "I think you said it earlier. You know too much. Too much for your own good, Reese. It can work against you. And I'm worried. You know what happens to whistle-blowers."

"Aw, Ward, you sound like a nursemaid. What can they possibly do?" He pointed to a black case still on the pier. "Hand me that too, will you?"

Ward shook his finger at Reese. "I'll tell you what they can do. Anything to shut you up, that's what! Like tie a hunk of concrete to your feet and drop you in the Tennessee River!"

"My God, Ward!" Reese scoffed. "That's a

47

little extreme, don't you think? The case, please."

Ward lifted the black case; something rattled inside. "What's this?"

"Just some vials. I'm going to take some samples of the lake while we're out today."

"Samples? What for?"

"To use as examples in my speech next weekend. I know the government keeps a close watch on the Chickamauga waterways, but I want to show the variance in chemical makeup from one area to another, even when it's closely monitored."

"Dang it, Reese, can't you forget about your chemicals long enough to go fishing for one day?" Ward stewed as he stepped down into the boat. "I thought we were going to have a relaxing day, doing nothing more strenuous than dipping our hooks to pull in a few bass."

"We are, Ward. This won't take much time. Or effort."

"While we've been standing here arguing, that old feller out there in the boat has pulled in three bigmouth bass! He'll have a whole mess before we get out on the lake."

"Not if you quit jawing and come on!"

"Wonder who the dickens he is . . ." Ward muttered as he took a seat.

Reese started the motor. As they passed the old fisherman, they waved and called, "Have a good day."

The old guy never lifted his head; he just waved and began winding in the line, another

48

bigmouth attached to the hook. The binoculars lay hidden beneath the seat.

Ward gave Reese directions to a secluded cove with fallen trees half hidden in the water, shaded by the leafy branches of trees lining the shore. "This is one of my favorite places to fish," Ward said quietly as he dropped his line in the water. "These dead tree trunks are just full of bass. And with the way they're biting today, we should have our limit before long."

"Remember, bass fishing is my specialty. I expect to get a whole string of them."

"Oh, yes. I'm banking on your fishing luck, Reese. It's been a long time since I've had time to sit and fish." Ward chuckled now and then as he talked. "You know, since I added those three additional cabins I've been so danged busy painting and fixing them up for the summer, I haven't had time for fishing. Had to go to Knoxville the other day to check on air-conditioning systems."

Reese nodded. "That reminds me. While you were away, I paid your cable TV bill. I have the receipt back at the cabin."

"Well, thank you, Reese, but you didn't have to do that."

"Oh, yes, I did. She told me you were two months late in your payments and she was supposed to cut it off if you didn't pay. So I took care of it for you. No big deal."

"I thought I paid that bill," Ward said with a puzzled look on his face. "I know I wasn't behind two months."

"You can clear it up with them later," Reese said nonchalantly, not wanting to embarrass his friend about not paying his bills.

"I could swear I paid that bill . . ." Ward mumbled.

Reese opened the case, drew out a couple of vials, took water samples, and labeled them.

There were no fish that day for Reese. His luck had gone sour. Tired and frustrated, they motored back and passed the same old fisherman floating aimlessly in the middle of the lake. No secluded cove. No fallen trees to provide good hiding places for bass. Still he pulled them in.

"You caught a good mess of 'em today, didn't you?" called Ward when they drew close.

The old man's boat bobbed in the waves created by their motor. His straw hat also bobbed as he nodded and waved. He was quite relieved that they kept going and didn't stop to chat and ask to see his string. There was no string of fish, because every one that grabbed the hook was tossed overboard as soon as possible.

As Reese and Ward tied up at the dock and began unloading their paraphernalia, the old fisherman started his motor and aimed for another dock along the shore. He secured his boat and hauled his weary body up the sloping bank, paid the dock attendant for the rental, and shuffled away.

"How'd you do?"

"No luck," the old man muttered.

50

"You mean my special silver-winged spinner bait didn't work for you?"

The old man shook his head and kept walking. How could he explain why he didn't have any fish? He didn't dare admit that every time he dropped the danged hook in the water, some poor fish—or maybe it was the *same* one —grabbed on to it!

The dock attendant scratched his head. "I'll be damned! That's the first time it didn't work!"

The grungy old fisherman climbed into his car and took off the ragged straw hat. Crushed black curls slowly sprang to life.

Tohni York, alias the grungy old fisherman, gazed into the rearview mirror at her reflection. "You are a wreck," she muttered. "And you smell like a can of tuna fish!" She started the car and drove back to her tiny cabin, wishing she had been able to monitor the conversations between Reese and his old friend Ward. Sometimes the discussion seemed a little heated, and she was dying to know what they argued about.

"Just keep him in sight" had been Joe's instructions.

Well, she'd kept him in sight all day. The only suspicious thing he'd done was to take several water samples. She was curious about that, but he'd admitted to Mandy at the restaurant that he was testing the lake. She wondered why, but it really wouldn't affect her job. It didn't

51

matter what he was doing. Only that she could get to him and bring him in when necessary.

Of all her days of bulldogging Reese Kreuger, this had been the most boring. She was glad when he and Ward had finally decided to pack it in, not just because she was weary of sitting still in a boat all day, but because she was tired of catching and releasing those danged fish! Fishing was not her sport, and she couldn't figure why the fish didn't realize that!

That night at the restaurant it was all she could do to serve fried catfish platters. Tohni kept seeing those fish she'd caught flopping around helplessly in the bottom of her boat.

She stopped by Reese's table. "Still studying, honey? You know, all this thinking might strain your brain," she quipped, and twisted an errant curl.

"Actually, I haven't been thinking all day, Mandy. Ward and I went fishing. I had hoped to net enough for a bass dinner tonight, but we didn't even catch one."

"Have you ever tried a silver-winged spinner?"

"No. What's that?"

"Well, it's this little thing about this long"—she measured with her fingers—"and it has little silver thingies dangling from it and it really works. Guaranteed to catch more fish than you'd know what to do with. Must be the shiny stuff that attracts the fish."

"How do you know that, Mandy? Do you like to fish?"

"Naw, I just listen to lots of fish tales around here." She laughed. "So you spent the day fishing, huh? Well, I'm proud of you, honey. Shows you can relax and get away from your notebooks once in a while."

"Mandy," Reese said, "whatever gave you the idea that I don't know how to have fun? Just because I read while I'm eating? That's to keep from being lonely."

"Does a lonely man really have fun?" she countered.

His blue eyes flickered and he shrugged. "I guess you got me, Mandy."

She smiled warmly. "Why, look at that, honey. You've been reading so hard, you broke your glasses!"

Reese laughed at her deduction. "They came apart at the hinge."

She picked them up and examined them. "Looks like you're missing a screw here. I'll bet I can fix that. Be right back."

Tohni sailed away to the kitchen. In less than ten minutes she returned and plunked the repaired glasses down on his notebook. "There! Good as new. Now you can go back to reading and being lonely."

"Why, Mandy, you're terrific. They *are* as good as new. How in the world did you manage that? Don't tell me you have a fix-it shop in the back room!"

She laughed. "You know I try to keep my

53

customers happy, Reese. Especially my regulars. There was an old pair of broken sunglasses on the kitchen windowsill. I just took the screw out of the hinge and installed it in yours."

"What a clever lady you are, Mandy. Thanks. You know, there seems to be no end to your talents."

She gave him a teasing smile. "I can also fix lonely hearts, honey, so if you ever need some female companionship, just call."

She started to walk away, but he grabbed her hand. "Okay. How about tomorrow, Mandy? Didn't I hear you tell a customer you were off tomorrow? I think it's going to be a very lonely day for me."

"W-well, no, I don't have to work tomorrow, Reese." Her gray eyes darkened. He was calling her bluff. After all this time, all the flirting, innuendos, and come-ons, Reese Kreuger was calling her bluff! *If you go fishing, be ready to net a big one!*

And how would Mandy Johnson respond to Reese's offer to go out with him on her day off? Tohni didn't even have to think twice. She cracked her gum and grinned. "What did you have in mind, sugar?"

He shrugged. "Haven't given it much thought. Just that I'd like to spend the day with you. You're right, it can be pretty lonely around here."

Tohni was a mass of confusion inside. Suddenly, she couldn't think of a single thing to say. Nor could she think of a way out. But why shouldn't she spend the day with Reese? After all, Joe had instructed her to keep an eye on Reese at all times.

"Why, I can't think of anybody I'd rather keep from being lonely, Reese."

"I thought you'd never say yes!"

"You just took me by surprise, honey."

"This won't get you in trouble, now, will it? Fraternizing with the customers."

She winked. "I won't tell if you won't." Ah, thank goodness Mandy Johnson was taking over. Tohni York felt like a stammering fool.

"How does a picnic sound? We can each bring a couple of dishes and take a boat over to some exotic island or abandoned beach."

"Sounds fine. Except you're in the wrong part of the country, honey. No beaches or exotic islands around here."

"Then we can pretend."

"Okay." She smiled. "I take back all my teasing. Maybe you do know how to have fun after all, Reese honey. What do you want me to bring to the picnic?"

"Let's make it pot luck. You bring along some favorites and I will too. That should make it easy for both of us."

"Now that sounds like a liberated picnic to me." Mandy giggled. "It's a deal. See you tomorrow. Uh . . . where?"

"I'm staying at Sutton's Lakeside Cabins. Why don't we meet there around eleven and we can take the boat right from the dock?"

"Sutton's," she repeated as if she didn't already know exactly where he lived. "Okay. See you then."

"And, Mandy . . ." He ran a finger sensuously over the back of her hand.

"Yes?" She tried to give him a questioning glance, although his gentle touch was like tingling fire on her hand.

"I'm in cabin three."

The woman in her took a trembling breath, and her eyes met his in a sparkling moment. "Okay. See you, Reese."

She tried to hide behind Mandy Johnson's facade as she sashayed across the restaurant, but Tohni York felt dizzy and weak-kneed at the thought of being alone with Reese all day.

Reese watched her move away to go about her job. With practiced ease she took up the coffeepot and began making the rounds. She smiled and teased at every table, leaving the women smiling and the men ogling. She had said her job was to make her customers happy, and that was exactly what she did. And for some damned, crazy reason, she made him happy too.

It was strange, because her type of woman usually didn't attract him. She was too flirty, too frivolous. Yet she had driven right to the core of his lonely heart. Maybe she was right and he was merely lonesome for female companionship. Maybe . . . oh, hell, maybe he just wanted to spend the day with Mandy Johnson. *And the night.* Reese left a generous tip on

56

the table and sauntered out, wishing tomorrow would come . . . and fast.

Tohni pocketed the generous tip with mixed feelings. This whole situation was so false, she hated it. Yet she couldn't back out. This wasn't the first time she had dated a subject, so what was the big deal? It would surely be more fun than sitting in a boat all day, observing Reese through binoculars. Or perched in a tree, watching him run. This would merely make her job easier. She could scrutinize Reese up close. What was so bad about that?

Tohni knew she was on the verge of losing the absolutely necessary detachment from her subject, one Reese Kreuger. She was far too excited about tomorrow, even though she realized it could be extremely risky to get involved in any way. So, she decided determinedly, she just wouldn't let herself think of him as a man —a man who excited her and made her feel all jittery inside. He was merely a subject, so don't be a fool, she warned herself. This case might be coming down by the weekend. Then there'll be no more contact with Mr. Reese Kreuger. You'll be finished with him.

But in her heart Tohni knew that what she wanted more than anything in the world was to spend the day with the man, to hear him talk, to make him laugh, to feel the touch of his hand . . . and that was dangerous thinking.

CHAPTER FOUR

Dangerous or not, Tohni headed for Sutton's pier the next morning with a certain bounce to her step, feeling an inescapable tingle of excitement. What better way to keep an eye on Mr. Kreuger than by staying at his side? Close enough to see the color of his eyes, to see that little dimple in his cheek, to talk and laugh and feel the warmth of his hand in hers. Heck, she'd wanted a closer look ever since she'd first spied him through the binoculars.

Carrying her brown paper bag of picnic surprises, Tohni smiled to herself and walked around back of the cabins, hoping to find Reese. She didn't. What she did see was the dock reaching out like a long gray finger into the lake—and a magnificent twenty-foot powerboat tied to the end of it.

Drawn like a honeybee to sweet clover, she walked out to the end of the pier, admiring the boat's sleek beauty and its saucy blue-and-white fishing canopy. It dwarfed the flat-bottomed fishing boats tied at the pier, and Tohni had to smile at the aptness of its name. *Brazen Beauty.*

"Now don't get excited. It isn't mine. I just rented it for the day."

"W-what?" She was astounded to see Reese's tanned face in the doorway under the bulk-head.

"Just for us. Well, come on aboard and check it out, Mandy. There's even a small galley with a refrigerator that makes ice."

Tohni almost gasped at the sight of him. Tanned to a golden brown, he looked extremely handsome in cutoff jeans and a copper-colored shirt. Suddenly, she was filled with trepidation that she wouldn't be able to continue the charade. Pretending to be a waitress named Mandy Johnson was too much like a lie. And while lying in the line of duty had never bothered her before, it seemed that looking Reese in the eye and lying was the most difficult thing she'd ever had to do. Frantically, she reminded herself that she had a job to do.

Getting a grip on herself, Tohni grinned, then giggled and slapped her thigh. "Well, I'll be a monkey's uncle! Reese Kreuger, is that you smack dab in the middle of that snazzy yacht? I always knew you were fancy! But this—?"

"Like it?" He moved across the deck, extending his hand to her. "Come aboard, Mandy. Today we can be fancy together. Step right here. Careful, now."

She beamed and took his hand, relishing the

feel of his firm grip. Oh, dear God, she thought, it was just beginning, this warmth, this natural familiarity. She had a whole day with Reese ahead of her and she wasn't at all sure she could handle it. To think of being near him, laughing, teasing, touching . . . Her old reservations returned.

"Jubilation T. Cornpone!" she exclaimed, tilting her head back to examine the canopy above. "If the folks from Fort Payne could see me now!"

"There you go again, thinking how you can use me to liven up your image," he teased. "Is this your picnic contribution?" He tried to take the paper bag from her while she oohed and ahhed over the covered deck. "Does any of this stuff need to be refrigerated?"

"Yes, but I'll do it." She held on to her package. "It's a surprise. Pot luck, remember?"

"I'll show you where to put things, then." He led the way into the tiny cabin.

Tohni's eyes traveled quickly from the stove on one side of the compact room to the bunk beds on the other. "Oh," she murmured weakly. "I see it's well-equipped."

"Sleeps six," he informed her, patting a bench. "This folds out into a double bed."

"Well, it beats a flat-bottomed fishing boat, which is what I expected today. You sure know how to impress a girl, Reese. Is that why you did this? To impress me?"

He hooked his thumbs into his back pockets. "Just thought we might enjoy it, that's all."

Tohni put her bag down on the counter. "Reese honey, I'll admit it. I'm impressed. I know I'm going to enjoy this to the max! Isn't that what they say out in California?"

"Me too, Mandy. But I couldn't care less what they say in California. I like you just the way you are. Southern and . . ."

Tohni smiled up at him, wishing she could read his thoughts and find out what he really thought of her. Of Mandy. But then it hardly mattered. If he knew who she really was, he'd probably dump her in the river and take off.

"And what?" she prodded.

"Sexy," he answered readily.

"Sexy? Me?" She smiled coyly while her heart skipped a beat. He certainly wasn't pulling any punches about what he expected today. *And just how do you handle this, cool, detached Ms. Tohni York?* "Why, I'm just a simple country girl, Reese."

"Sometimes country girls are the best, Mandy."

Best at what? she wondered. *Deceiving?*

Tohni hadn't realized how tiny the cabin was and how closely they stood until she felt his energy and faintly smelled his appealing male scent. Inexorably, she felt drawn by his strong aura. Oh, dear God, this *was* dangerous. After all, she was only a woman, entirely vulnerable to his masculine charms.

Trying to sound casual, she asked, "Reese honey, can you make this boat move? We don't want to stand here all day staring into each other's eyes, do we? By the way, you have very nice eyes. Kind of silvery blue in this light."

He moved closer to her. "Do you realize this is the first time I've seen you in anything but your uniform, Mandy? You look . . . different. But good. Very good."

She lifted her arms and began to twirl. "I wore my best jeans today . . ." By the time she'd finished turning around for him, he had pulled her into his arms. "Just for you, Reese honey. . . ." She finished weakly as his arms drew her into the fork of his legs. His strong thighs clamped firmly on hers.

"I like the way you look, Mandy," he murmured, lowering his lips for a deliberate kiss. The touch of his warm, velvety lips made her head spin.

She leaned—or did he pull her—against the hard planes of his golden body and she felt the strength of his arms and legs encircling her. His pelvis thrust forward in a masculine gesture and she responded by tilting her own hips ever so slightly.

Oh, dear, she thought. I have to stop this before it goes any further. Lifting her head quickly, she cooed, "Oh, Reese honey, for a deep thinker you sure know how to kiss."

"I've been thinking about kissing you for days. You inspire feelings in me I haven't felt in a long time."

She lowered her eyes. "Those feelings are called lust, honey. And they're caused by loneliness."

"Maybe you're right, Mandy. But it certainly feels good when I hold you close like this. I can feel the loneliness slide away." His large hands ran down the sides of her body from the sensitive area beside her breasts to her ribs, to her waist and hips. When his hands reached her rounded buttocks he pulled her against him again. "See? Nice . . . and inviting." His lips captured hers; it was all she could do to push him away.

"When you asked me aboard this little yacht, I thought we'd at least leave the dock, Reese. Now how can I brag to my friends in Fort Payne if we don't go anywhere?"

Her laughter was slightly nervous. She'd have to work on that. Mandy shouldn't be jittery. She should be enjoying this close encounter with Reese Kreuger, even if Tohni York was a nervous wreck.

"You could tell them we had a wonderful day trying out the beds in the cabin," he suggested with a wicked smile.

"No!" she protested a little too quickly. "That is, not right now, honey. I want to see if this baby will run. And how fast. Come on, Reese. I've never been on a yacht before."

"It isn't a yacht. It's a pleasure craft. Let's make it pleasurable, Mandy." His hands covered her breasts and pressed gently into their softness.

She muffled a small moan, and then managed to sound reasonably light. "Just being with you is pleasurable enough, Reese honey.

But you promised me an exotic island. A beach. And a picnic. That means food. It's no fun having a picnic on a boat that's tied to a dock."

"Maybe not, but I can show you what *is* fun, whether tied to a dock or not."

"Reese—"

"Mandy . . ." he murmured as his thumbs rubbed her nipples. "Feel that? You want me too."

With great effort she pulled away from him. Her gray eyes looked at him steadily. "Why did you bother to rent the boat," she asked, "if this was all you wanted?"

"Are you trying to deny it's what you want too?"

"Reese, I . . ." She was on the verge of telling him who she really was and what she really wanted from him, but her instincts told her *not now!*

"Okay, Mandy. You don't have to explain. But I know there's something between us, so don't lie to yourself."

Tohni gasped at the truth of his statement. Intuitively, he'd driven right to the heart of the situation. What he didn't know was that everything about her was a lie and that she already hated herself for misleading him.

"Now don't get angry, Reese honey," she managed to murmur. "It's early yet. This is supposed to be a day for fun, not arguing. I'll just put my stuff in the fridge here. Then I'd like to drive this baby. How can I brag about driving a yacht if I never get behind the wheel?"

His eyes flickered as he realized she was maneuvering him. But the angry flash dwindled quickly. He had all day, so he might as well take his time with this very appealing but highly unpredictable woman. "I don't want you to think you've missed anything that might be fun, Mandy."

She turned to face him with her hands on her hips. Her smile showed her honest relief at his decision to back off. "Reese honey, I don't get a chance to go with many fancy fellows. And you'll be gone before I know it. You can't blame me for taking advantage of every opportunity that arises. Like spending a whole day with you and driving this yacht."

His electric-blue eyes danced as he threw his hands up. "Taking advantage of me and admitting it yet! You're a silver-tongued pixie, Mandy, but I love your determination. And your surprises. What next?"

"Next? Start the motor, captain. I'll be right up."

"That sounds like my line," he muttered with a grin, and shuffled out.

"Up on *deck!*" she called, laughing.

Joining him, Tohni kept one hand behind her back and gave him a teasing grin. "I have something for you."

"Now that's more like it," he said with a sexy grin. "I'm glad you've come to your senses."

"This is for you." She brought her hand

around and extended an outstretched palm. In it lay a strange-looking shiny silver object.

"What is *that?*"

"It's a silver-winged spinner, guaranteed to catch as many fish as you can handle."

He eyed the item curiously. "And I've wanted one for so long."

"Hey!" She snatched her hand back. "If you don't appreciate it, there are plenty of fellows who would love to have one of these."

"One of these?" he asked, lifting the glittering object. "Or one of these?" He placed a kiss right in the center of her palm.

Tohni gasped as tiny tingles of delight spread all through her. "Reese!"

He slid his arm around her. "I love the spinner, Mandy. It's probably one of the most, uh, useful gifts I've ever received. I think there may be a couple of fishing rods on board and we can try it out later if you want to. Right now, let's drive this boat away from the dock without running into anything."

Standing in the circle of his arms and feeling as snug and secure as a bug in a rug, Tohni helped Reese steer the boat. He placed his hands over hers on the wheel and together they maneuvered the craft out into the middle of the lake, heading straight for paradise. The wind tossed Tohni's black curls and caressed her cheeks as she leaned against Reese's strong chest. She wished they could stay that way forever.

Reese's lips brushed her earlobe with occasional kisses and Tohni smiled to herself, enjoying every moment. *Oh, Mandy, eat your heart out! I've got him right where I want him. Close to me!*

As they drew near a bank lined with pine trees, Reese called, "One exotic isle coming up! You hold to while I drop anchor."

"Hey, you're picking up this nautical lingo pretty good."

Reese saluted and disappeared. For a moment Tohni felt cold and lonely. One thing was for sure: She liked the feel of his arms around her—liked it all too well.

The craft bobbed gently about twelve feet offshore. They stood on deck for a minute, assessing the shoreline.

"Well, we have two choices," Reese decided. "We can stay on board and have our picnic here, or we can wade ashore, balancing our lunch on our heads, and eat among the ants."

"That's an easy choice. I vote for eating here under the blue-and-white canopy. Wading and balancing and fighting ants don't sound appealing to me. Maybe we can wade in later."

"This girl has a sensible head on her shoulders." He nodded in agreement. "To the canopy then, m'lady."

Tohni found a blanket and brought out her bag of goodies for their lunch. Reese joined her. "Aren't you going to share what you brought?"

"You first," she insisted.

"I hope we didn't both bring the same

thing." He grinned sheepishly. "With you being a southern lady, I figured you would want to show off your culinary skills, while I, being not-so-southern, still like a dish that you probably cook very well. But I thought you might not have time to fix it, so since I love it . . ."

"Get on with it, will you!"

"I brought my favorite anyway." He took from a bag a huge colorful plastic bucket of fried chicken and set it in the middle of the blanket.

She rolled with laughter. "What culinary skills did you exercise in buying that chicken?"

"Ah, knowing where to buy is half the battle. I discovered early on that the Colonel fixes the best fried chicken in town. Now it's your turn."

"You'll see that we make a good team. I, too, know something about the art of buying," Tohni said, slyly taking out her first item. She set the bottle of wine beside the chicken, then handed Reese a corkscrew. "I'll let you do the honors." She got out two plastic wineglasses and dug into the bag again.

"There's more?"

"Oh, my, yes!" She smiled and named each item as she added it to their spread. "Pickled pigs' feet, an old southern favorite."

"Argh!" he groaned loudly.

"Don't knock it 'til you've tried it! And smoked octopus."

"Octopus? Mandy!"

"Well, I thought a fancy man like yourself might have developed a taste for such refined fare." She placed the jars side by side. "Then there's pickled cauliflower. Pickled okra. They're hot," she warned. "But delicious."

Skeptically, he watched her.

"And the chef's choice, marinated artichoke hearts. Hmm, Reese, wait'll you try these. They're great."

"Can't wait, Mandy."

"And last but not least, potato chips."

"Something as ordinary as potato chips with all this exotic food?"

"Sour-cream flavored. There! All my favorites!" she said with satisfaction. "And they all go perfectly with fried chicken."

He gazed at her in amazement. "Mandy, what would we have eaten if I hadn't brought something substantial?"

"Octopus and okra," she answered breezily. "Don't forget I'm a working girl, Reese. I didn't have much time to prepare for this feast. Honestly, I'm not much of a cook." She was struck with the realization that this was one of the few times she'd actually been honest with him.

"What?" He feigned shock. "A southern girl who can't cook? That's okay, Mandy, I understand. I'm not such a great cook myself."

She smiled with appreciation at this golden man who was so understanding. God, he was practically perfect! How could she admit to him that her mother always had a maid who did the cooking for them?

"Then you aren't disappointed that I didn't

do anything special?" Tohni lifted her gray eyes questioningly to his. Crazily, at that moment she wished Stella had taught her to make something special. Like chocolate cake—or fried chicken.

Reese took her hand and the warmth of his touch sent her emotions spiraling. "All this is special, Mandy. Just like you." His lips played sensuously along her knuckles. "I'm lucky to be able to spend today with you."

"You make it sound like you might be gone tomorrow, Reese."

"I might."

Not unless it's with me! Tohni thought, but asked innocently, "Why? Where will you go, Reese honey?"

"Circumstances beyond my control, Mandy."

"You don't want to talk about it, do you?"

"You're right." He raised his wineglass. "To you, Mandy. A special—and surprising—lady."

"To a day on an exotic island with a thinking man who likes fried chicken." She raised her glass with a sad smile. It was almost as if they were toasting to the one and only time they'd be together, and that was, indeed, a sad thought.

But this was also a day for pretending, and Tohni could imagine that she was someone else. Someone Reese cared for. She could imagine that they would be together like this indefinitely. Her laughter tinkled like bells under the blue-and-white canopy and scattered on the wind to their make-believe exotic island.

She opened the jar of artichoke hearts and popped one into her mouth. "Hmm, great! You try this one." She picked out another with her fingers and fed it to him.

Laughing, he pulled her close and took her offering; then, in a purely sensual act, he held her hand until he had licked each finger completely clean.

By the time he'd finished, Tohni was utterly and completely weak. "I forgot forks," she muttered inanely when he was done. "I'm sure there must be some in the galley."

He clutched her, not allowing her to go. "It's much more fun eating with our fingers. Especially *your* fingers. They taste marvelous. Anyway, who are we trying to impress?"

She grinned, happiness surging through her. "Maybe you're right. This isn't a day for forks."

Indeed, it wasn't a day for the civility of eating with forks, nor of trying to impress, nor of doing anything but enjoying simple pleasures. Tohni relaxed and let the uninhibited Mandy Johnson take over and relish every moment with Reese.

She told herself repeatedly that she could easily go home at the end of the day and forget Reese. They laughed and teased and fed each other the unusual foods she had brought, then devoured nearly all of the crusty fried chicken.

When they'd finished they waded ashore to explore the small Tennessee jungle on the island. The "exotic" island proved devoid of succulent fruit, hidden caves, buried treasure, or natives. There weren't even any nice beaches on which to sprawl in the sun. So after trekking its two mile perimeter, they helped each other back aboard and fell exhaustedly on deck.

Tohni glanced at their feet and shrieked, "Eek! Look at our muddy tennis shoes! We'll ruin the deck!"

"Hold 'em right there," Reese instructed, peeling his off. "We'll set them in the sun to dry, then we can just knock the mud off into the river."

"That's a thinking man for you," Tohni quipped, lifting her feet so Reese could remove her shoes. "A solution for every problem."

He discarded the muddy shoes and caressed her bare feet. It was a disturbingly sensual sensation, his hands massaging her tired arches, spreading her toes apart, slowly rotating her ankles. His deft hands slipped into her damp jeans, reaching for the tight muscles of her calves. "You have nice legs, Mandy."

"And you have nice hands, Reese honey. I hate to break this up, but I'm dying of thirst! Is there any ice water in the fridge?"

Reluctantly, Reese lowered her legs, then stood and pulled her to her feet. "You don't expect to cool things down with a little ice water, do you?" he chided.

Tohni just cast him an impish smile and headed for the galley.

Reese followed, fully aware that, although

they had worked up a thirst on their little outing, this was definitely an evasion tactic.

Eventually, they settled into separate activities on the boat. Reese tried out the new fishing lure from the stern. Tohni shed her jeans, wet and muddy from their excursion, and hung them over the side of the boat to dry in the sun. Later she realized that it was something the practical Tohni York would do, as well as prudently wearing a swimsuit under her jeans and T-shirt. Not that Tohni was the least bit self-conscious about her body. But perhaps she should have been.

There was a nice easy feeling between them as the day wore on. Tohni hauled a pillow from the cabin, placed it on the blanket on deck, and settled down to watch Reese fish from the back of the craft. That was her job, wasn't it? Watching Reese Kreuger. And what a thoroughly enjoyable job it was too.

The food, wine, and midday warmth combined to lull her enticingly. Tohni's eyelids grew heavy. Relaxed, floating, watching the gorgeous golden body of Reese Kreuger, the day became dreamlike. A beautiful, erotic dream in which she was honest about who she was and how she felt. In a misty fantasy he took her in his arms and they made wild, passionate love while the waves lapped softly at the sides of the boat. They drifted away from the real world. Away from her job. Away from the people who were looking for him. They drew closer and his lips captured hers . . .

"Wa-hoo!"

Tohni was jolted to a sitting position, adrenaline shooting through her veins.

"Hot damn! This is the greatest little fishing lure I've ever seen, Mandy! I've caught four fish in the last hour!"

"I hope you let them all go," she mumbled, trying to get her bearings after being awakened so abruptly, trying to dismiss her ridiculous dream.

"Let them go? Are you crazy? We can have a mess of fish some night for supper."

"Ugh!"

"I thought you liked fish."

"I do," she added hastily, remembering that Mandy had tempted him with her favorite fish recipe. "But, uh, cleaning fish is not my idea of ending a perfect day."

"What is?" He paused, and when she didn't answer right away, he added, "How does trout amandine sound?"

"Better." She nodded. "Are you fixing?"

"Yep. It's back at the cabin, ready to pop in the oven. Leaves us plenty of time for . . . uh, whatever."

"Sounds like you have tonight planned too."

"Not really. I'd rather relax and let nature take its course. The day isn't over yet, Mandy."

He meant it as a promise, but Tohni took it as a warning. She pushed her hair back and decided she must be crazy to put herself in a position like this all day long with Reese. Now she was even dreaming about the guy! She slumped back down and let her deep gray eyes wander over him. He'd removed his shirt and was a golden dream of tight muscle and lean sinew.

He stashed the fishing rod and placed the fish he'd caught on ice down in the galley. Tohni could hear him inside the cabin then, washing his hands and rummaging in the fridge. He whistled happily, the sound alluring to her.

When Reese returned he handed her a Seven-Up and heaved his large, angular body down on the blanket beside her. Tohni was acutely aware that she wore only a swimsuit under her short T-shirt and that he wore only cutoffs. Her jeans still hung over the railing, and she longed for their protection for her bare legs.

The Tohni in her felt uneasy that Reese was so close, so familiar. But Mandy was wickedly delighted to have his shirtless body within easy reach. She struggled for control. Sighing, she decided to relinquish this moment to Mandy. After all, that's who he thought he was getting. Why not humor him? And herself.

Her eyes traveled traitorously over his muscular thighs, noticing the pattern of sandy, curly hair on his tanned legs. "There's some wine left from lunch," she said.

"No thanks." He stretched out his long legs and they extended beyond the edge of the blanket. One thigh rested against hers, casually. And it sent her blood racing.

"Don't you like wine?"

"Sure. I had a glass at lunch. I don't need more."

"And apparently you aren't a beer drinker either."

"Nope. Not much."

Tohni raised up on one elbow and took a gulp of the Seven-Up he'd placed between them. "I like something with a little more punch to it myself. Go for the gusto, I always say."

"My mother says that too. She goes for the gusto to escape reality. Not a pretty sight in an otherwise attractive woman."

"Does she have a drinking problem?" Tohni pursed her lips. There'd been no mention in his file that his mother was an alcoholic.

"Hell, I don't know why I told you that, Mandy." His face grew tight, and she watched a tiny muscle quiver in his cheek.

"Why, Reese honey, I'm glad you did. It helps me know you better. It means you trust me with your family secrets. I like that."

His hand trailed down the length of her arm, sending tingles over her skin. "Mandy, I've needed a day like this. To relax. And enjoy. And share with someone who doesn't make judgments. It means a lot to me."

"Is that a lonely man talking?"

"Is this a lonely lady responding?" His hand slid over the slickness of her swimsuit, cupping her breast. His thumb rubbed the nipple and she responded all the way down to her toes. Could he tell that too?

She moved jerkily. "Reese honey, you send shivers down my spine when you do that."

He leaned back, no longer touching her, and she was immediately sorry. His voice was low and sensuous. "What are you doing here, Mandy, working at the Catfish King? Waiting for Mr. Right to come along?"

"I don't believe in Mr. Right. I can take care of myself."

"That attitude sounds pretty liberated for a pretty little southern gal. I must admit, I'm surprised at that. You know, you've surprised me in many ways today. You seem different from the flirty little woman who works at the Catfish King."

"Oh, no, I'm not," she responded quickly. "Same person, Reese." Tohni had feared she couldn't keep up the facade of Mandy Johnson all day. Maybe she *was* slipping.

He propped himself on one elbow and examined her closely. "I can't quite figure you out. A girl from Alabama with exotic tastes like smoked octopus and artichoke hearts?"

"Sure. Why not?" She giggled, but felt a little nervous inside. "You forgot about the pickled pigs' feet!"

"Hmm, that brands you as southern, all right. There are times, though, when I think there's another Mandy here. A Mandy who has lived other places, had broader experiences, met different kinds of people. Someone who belongs somewhere else."

Her heart pounded at his insight, but her

response was purposeful and light. "Oh, Reese honey, it's because I read a lot. I don't want to miss a thing in this world and would dearly love to travel. Now you know my deepest secret."

His fingers played along her chin and turned it to his face. "Somehow, Mandy, I don't think you've missed a thing along the way. Like right now. Here we are together, both changing. Both our lives in turmoil. Both of us lonely . . ." His hand moved slowly to her breast, his thumb moving continuously over the firm nipple beneath the nylon of her swimsuit. "Mandy, I want to know all about you. All your secrets. We could make this day perfect. Just us two . . ."

Tohni fought for supremacy as she felt herself slipping farther into the glorious oblivion of Reese's presence. But as his hand traveled over the feminine recesses and curves of her body, so scantily clad, Mandy took over, allowing her to enjoy his sensuous, masculine touch. She thrilled at his closeness. Their legs brushed, his thigh pressing against hers, his calf crossing over hers.

She struggled in protest. "Reese honey, I do like you. A lot. But we're very different, you and me."

"Not so different, Mandy." He turned her body toward his. "We want the same things. Each other." His lips met hers gently in a series of sweet, sensuous kisses; then he peppered

78

her cheeks and eyelids with kisses and teased her lips open with darting forays of his tongue.

Tohni could feel herself weakening, falling into his masculine trap, wanting to set loose her feminine self, to experience Reese Kreuger to the fullest. "No, Reese," she said in a whisper. "You've got me wrong. I don't—"

"You're lying, Mandy. You do want me." His hand traveled lightly over her bare leg, moving to the sensitive flesh of her inner thigh. "Don't pretend with me. I can feel your reaction. I'm dying for you. Surely you know that."

She swallowed hard. "Well, sure, honey, I know what you're . . . uh, I know about that. But I, well, I hate to give in to a guy who's going to be gone so soon. You said maybe tomorrow. Is that fair?"

Was any of this fair? she thought crazily. Was she playing fair with him?

His fingers played over her thigh and along the edge of her bathing suit, slipping inside it occasionally. "Oh, God, Mandy, you're so soft and sweet, you're impossible to resist!"

She felt a flood of warmth surge through her body, betraying her.

His large hands moved up her tight suit to slide inside and cup each firm breast. Inexorably, she arched to the touch and he kissed her long and hard. When his tongue probed her lips, imploring, she opened eagerly to receive him further.

The warm strength of his tongue touched hers and Tohni almost cried aloud, *Mandy, help me out of this!* She felt herself slipping away to the seductive joy of Reese's entreaties. Slipping fast to commit the unforgivable! To let herself become personally involved with a subject! This wasn't like her at all! She had never allowed this to happen. So why couldn't she get control of the situation?

Maybe you don't want to be in control!

His eyes were dark with passion as he scattered kisses over the creamy swells of her breasts. He lifted her breasts from their confinement and blessed each rosy nipple with a kiss.

"Reese, oh, Reese, no—"

"Mandy, can't we just enjoy the present and each other with no commitments? I've had an unpleasant relationship and no doubt you have too. There's no sense rushing into another. Let's make this good, just for today. We're both lonely and we're attracted to each other."

"Reese honey, you make it so hard to resist you." She took a deep breath and placed her hands on his bare chest, intending to push him away. Instead her hands defied her head and spread over the hard masculine planes and beautifully rounded muscles. Her fingertips ran over his nipples and along his ribs to his back.

Taking that as acceptance, Reese pressed his body to hers. "Don't deny this, Mandy. For either of us. We need each other."

"Need? Oh, Reese, don't . . ."

"We need each other today."

"But what about tomorrow? Will you be gone, Reese?"

"We'll deal with that tomorrow. Oh, God, Mandy, I want you. Your touch is like magic to me."

"Ma-magic?" Tohni tried to think straight. This went against every fiber in her, against her personal code for conducting relationships, her vow to remain detached from her subjects. But Reese Kreuger was different. From the first he'd captured her imagination. Her fantasy. And now her wildest fantasy could come true. He was here; so was she. They each desired the other, but deep in her heart she knew it would be wrong to let her fantasy become reality.

"Reese," she groaned, summoning every ounce of willpower she had. "Please stop. Please!"

CHAPTER FIVE

Tohni curled away from Reese and rocked as if in agony. They had come so close, *so close*, to disaster. Or was it paradise? Regardless, it was over.

She had done what she had to do. Not what Mandy Johnson, the flirty waitress, would have done. Not even what Tohni York, the woman, would have done. But what was required of Tohni York, the private investigator.

With an angry groan Reese lunged to his feet. He stood at the boat's stern, looking over the lake.

Tohni sat up and gazed at his back, so straight and muscular and golden. He was beautiful in a strong masculine way and she'd wanted him. He'd wanted her too.

Reese moved to the helm and brought the engine to life. They rode back to shore in silence.

"Grab the rope, will you?"

Tohni's hands shook as she looped the hemp rope around the dock post. Through misty gray eyes she watched the man who, until a few hours ago, had been only a subject, someone to watch. Someone on whom to report back to Joe. Now the situation was different. She had allowed herself to become involved, if not physically then certainly emotionally. Her stomach churned with turmoil.

What would she say to Joe? *Oh, yes, I'm keeping Kreuger in sight at all times. Also in my arms. Incidently, he knows all the right moves.*

She ran a nervous hand over her forehead. Worse yet, she had deceived Reese. He thought she was one woman when really she was quite another. A devious one. A double-dealer. An informer.

She could hear herself stumbling over the words in explanation: *Reese honey, I'm not really Mandy Johnson, sweet southern lady from Fort Payne, Alabama. I'm not even honest. I'm Tohni York, a cool and treacherous private eye. I've been watching you for weeks. Lying to you. And wanting you.* She shuddered at the mental picture of his reaction. Oh, God, she didn't want to see that. And yet she knew she would, sooner or later.

Where was the cool Tohni York now?

"Hey, Mandy, are you with the program? Want to help me here?"

"Sure, Reese." She stumbled around, cleaning up the boat and gathering their picnic supplies. She tucked the blanket under her arm and Reese grabbed the string of fish.

They avoided meeting each other's eyes, and

83

their strained voices betrayed the tension between them. They spoke only when necessary. What was there to say?

Tohni stood by while Reese paid the dock manager for use of the boat. Then he handed the man the string of fish. When they were out of earshot she asked, "You didn't want to keep those bass?"

"You were right, Mandy. They're too much trouble to clean." He cleared his throat and asked, "Are you going to stay for trout amandine tonight?"

"I think not," she answered weakly. She couldn't tolerate another hour of close contact with Reese. The tension between them was already so strong she could feel it. Oh, dear God, how long could she continue this charade?

"I figured as much," he replied sullenly.

"I'm sorry, Reese. It's just that I don't think I can stay for dinner, as much as I'd like to. I . . . I have other plans. I hope you understand."

"I understand all right," he answered tightly.

They rode in silence back to his cabin where her car was parked. Tohni got out and stood clumsily between the two cars. She wanted to say something to smooth everything out, but couldn't find the words. Reese slammed his car door and ambled over, his fists shoved into the pockets of his cutoffs.

"It's been a beautiful day, Reese honey," she

said, attempting Mandy's voice. "That boat was wonderful. Something to write home about."

"I'm glad I entertained you," he muttered sardonically.

She met his gaze with cold, gray defiance. "I didn't go along to entertain you, Reese. And I certainly didn't expect that from you."

His blue eyes swept over her with disdain. "You're nothing but a tease, Mandy. You've been flaunting yourself around me for days in that restaurant. You even suggested a romantic evening like the one I planned for tonight. It was your idea!"

Tohni lowered her eyes. "I'm sorry, Reese honey. Maybe . . . maybe next time." She struggled with the raging torrent inside her, knowing there wouldn't—couldn't—be a next time. And yet Tohni knew he was right. She had teased and taunted him as Mandy Johnson, not dreaming it would ever come to this. That she would ever have to make good on her seductive body language.

They exchanged curt good-byes and Tohni drove away.

Even as she left him in anger she couldn't help wondering how to win back his confidence. Patch up their differences. By going to bed with him? If it were that simple, she'd fly back and throw herself into his arms. But it was more than that. She'd used him. And deceived him. That was something she'd have to live with. And the worst was yet to come. *When she turned him in.*

She was convinced he only wanted her for sex. There was nothing more to their relationship than lust. He was still the playboy, still the globe-trotting womanizer. Only now he was hiding out, forced into a small corner of Tennessee, so he was willing to use the only female within reach to satisfy his baser needs. And briefly, she'd been all too willing. Thank God she had come to her senses in time.

He didn't give a damn about Mandy Johnson. He only wanted to use her. That realization hurt more than Tohni wanted to admit.

Before going to her temporary abode, she stopped at the familiar pay phone next to the all-night grocery store.

"Joe? How much longer?"

"Hang in there, kid. Maybe a couple of days. Then it'll all be over and you can come back home. What's wrong? Tennessee getting to you?"

"Yeah, you could say that, Joe."

He paused. "Is everything all right, Tohni? Kreuger isn't giving you any trouble, is he?"

"Oh, no. No trouble. Uh, Joe, tell me more about this Ansel Corporation. Are they legitimate? And honest? Why are they after Kreuger?"

"They're just about the biggest waste disposal company on the entire East Coast. We're talking big bucks, kid. Are they legit? They've got government contracts, the whole works."

"If they're so big, why are they bothering with Kreuger?"

Joe drew a quick breath. "Ansel's probably after alimony for his daughter, like all the rest of our clients. Anyway, it doesn't matter. That's something you don't need to know. Just do your job."

"I don't think it's alimony. Doesn't fit in."

"Tohni—"

"Okay, Joe. Okay. I'll check in tomorrow. Thanks." Tohni hung up the phone feeling more heartsick than before. Why on earth did she thank him? Thanks for making me miserable! Thanks for giving me this particular assignment and getting me involved with Reese Kreuger! Thanks for nothing, Joe!

Damn! She was blaming Joe as if it were his fault! She could only blame herself. Not Joe. Not even Reese. She'd gotten herself into this mess. And she would have to work her way out of it. But why did she feel so rotten?

Strangely, a lump the size of a fist formed in her throat. She wanted to end this, wanted to tell Mr. Kreuger the truth, wanted to go home. She dashed unbidden tears from her gray eyes and rushed inside the grocery store. She had a feeling that tonight she'd need a full bag of sour cream potato chips.

In a daze Tohni let herself into her small rented cabin and paced the floor, gazing about the familiar room as if she'd never seen the place before. What was she doing here? What had she set herself up for? Tohni York had never felt so distraught over a case. For the first time ever, Tohni had gotten herself deeply involved with a subject. They'd almost—*almost* —made love. Worse yet, she'd been insanely tempted to give in to their passion! Her feelings for Reese ran stronger than her desire to control her actions.

She threw herself into bed and stared at the ceiling. Her eyes grew misty and for the first time—ever—Tohni York cried about a case.

Reese Kreuger slept fitfully. Finally, at barely four in the morning, he was drinking coffee and staring from the pier into the black waters of Chickamauga Lake.

He'd acted like a fool and needed no one to tell him. But Mandy frustrated him so much, tantalizing and teasing her way into his life, then lifting her perky nose and turning away from him. When he'd realized she didn't intend to carry through on her unspoken promises, he'd been furious. He'd reacted badly. As sweet as she seemed on the surface, he knew her well enough to bet that Mandy Johnson didn't go lightly into any relationship. Especially one that promised little more than a brief sexual encounter.

He could still see the glint of stubborn determination in her eyes. But they'd been as soft as a kitten's when he'd kissed her.

And now that he'd felt her softness, known the sweetness of her lips, that's all he could think of. He wouldn't rest until he felt her in his arms again.

Oh, God! That's nonsense! He gulped the remaining coffee and headed back to the cabin for more. He'd had other women, plenty of them. And sexier too. So what was it with this pixie-faced woman? Was he attracted to her just because he was lonely? Probably.

He sloshed more black coffee into his mug and the dark liquid danced with her image. Haunting gray eyes. Bouncy curls that melted like froth between his fingers. Lips that smiled saucily and dared his invasion. Small, firm ruby-tipped breasts begging to be touched . . . and kissed.

What was so special about this woman? Nothing. She wasn't even his type. But then who *was* his type? Maybe he was changing. Everything about Mandy intrigued him. But he still had the niggling feeling she wasn't revealing everything to him. That she was hiding a secret past. Well, who wasn't hiding something?

Hell, she was right. He'd be gone in a week. Maybe less. And probably wouldn't see her again after that. Well, the very least he could do was apologize for his boorish behavior. Today. Before she reported to work. He'd tell her . . . what? That he wanted her with a burning desire that kept him awake half the night? That he was fighting a losing battle with the corporate establishment? That he might end up at the bottom of the Tennessee River if he wasn't careful?

He ran a hand over the rugged planes of his

face. Maybe he'd simply tell her he wanted to see her smile again. That's all.

By five A.M. Reese was jogging on false energy generated by too much coffee. By noon he was completely frustrated because he couldn't find her. It seemed that no one at work knew Mandy Johnson or where she lived.

"I've looked everywhere for you!" He met her car as she pulled into the back parking lot of the Catfish King. "It's crazy, but after all this time I don't know where you live, Mandy."

She carefully avoided his dark blue gaze. "Oh? I can't imagine why you'd need to know."

"Don't play coy, Mandy. I'm tired of your games. And I . . . want to apologize."

She opened the car door, still avoiding his eyes. "For what?"

His arm shot out, braced against the doorframe, effectively blocking her way. "For my behavior. I came on too strong. I realize that now."

She lifted her chin, hoping the red in her eyes wasn't too noticeable. "Why, Reese honey, I thought that's the way you always were. Used to having your way about everything."

"Damn it, Mandy." He shifted uncomfortably. "Maybe . . . maybe that's how it looks to you, but it's not that way. I didn't mean to scare you off."

"You didn't scare me. I just had to leave,

Reese. Things . . . things were happening too fast."

"Mandy, I *don't* apologize for wanting you. I can't help that. I'm only a man. And you're . . . you're a very attractive woman."

She tossed her dark curls and the perky waitress's cap shifted. "It was kind of nice, Reese honey, your finding me attractive. Until you got other ideas in your head."

His blue gaze intensified. "I want to see you again, Mandy. Tonight."

She shook her head, grateful that work provided a legitimate excuse to avoid him. "Sorry, Reese. I have to work late."

"Tomorrow, then."

"I have to work overtime tomorrow night. Some private banquet for political people— senators and such. It must be something special because they've flown in lobsters for the occasion."

He sighed and looked away, then back at her. There was some embarrassment in his tone. "I'm speaking to the group tomorrow night, Mandy. Here. At the Catfish King."

She laughed in disbelief. "You?"

He sighed again. How could he explain his strange business to her? Certainly not here. Not now. "Later, Mandy. After the banquet. I have to see you."

"Reese, you aren't kidding, are you?"

"No, Mandy. I want to see you afterward. We have a lot to talk about."

"I mean, you're serious about speaking tomorrow night. What in the world are you going to speak on, Reese honey? That stuff you've been studying? Garbage?"

"You might say that. Contaminated ground water. Chemical-dump seepage. Toxic waste. The environment."

"Huh?" She reached up and brushed his cheek with gentle fingertips. "Reese honey, what kind of man have I gotten myself involved with? You sound so serious. I thought you were just real snazzy. A spoiled rich dude, always expecting to have things his way."

His jaw tightened at her touch. "I told you there are things about me you don't know, and probably couldn't understand. Sometimes I don't understand myself."

Tohni looked at him, feeling a funny tingling inside. It wasn't so much his words, which were strange enough. But his tone, so . . . distressed, almost desperate. He'd touched a chord within her. Maybe he knew he could maneuver her this way. But she didn't care. Right now she only cared about him. About Reese Kreuger, the man.

"Sure, Reese. We could talk about it tomorrow night. After the banquet. Now, are you going to move so I can get to work before I get fired?"

He bent down and kissed her lips quickly. Instantly, sparks of something strong and overwhelming rekindled between them. It was there, almost tangible, for both of them to feel.

She smiled and sighed softly. Touching his golden cheek gently, she walked away.

Against her better judgment, Tohni looked forward to seeing Reese tomorrow night after the banquet.

CHAPTER SIX

Tohni was assigned to the head table for the banquet, and before the evening was complete, she'd developed a great respect for waitresses. Her feet ached and her head spun as she tried to please her finicky customers. The coffee was cold; cream floated on top. The tea was too hot, melted the ice. The baked potato was cold, wouldn't melt the butter. Someone dropped his fork. More tea. Could she replace this spilled martini? And mop it up, please? Remove the salads. Bring the plates. Remove the plates. Bring the dessert. Refill the coffee cups. Whew!

She leaned against the kitchen wall and moaned, "Aren't they finished eating yet?"

"Soon. Very soon. Make sure everyone has coffee refills before the speaker starts," her boss directed.

She whisked out again, brandishing a steaming pot of coffee, and proceeded to refill every cup in her area whether the customer wanted coffee or not.

Reese tried not to notice Mandy. He glanced

at his notes in a futile effort to redirect his thoughts. But he couldn't help but admire the way her pert breasts thrust above the vest that was laced tightly against her ribs. He knew how those breasts felt against his palms and he ached to touch her again. His wicked eyes observed her short skirt edging farther up her shapely thighs when she stretched to pour the coffee.

What a flirt she was. And a tease. But he'd discovered that her promises were idle. Even knowing that, he couldn't wait to be alone with her tonight.

Finally everyone was fed. Every coffee cup refilled. Reese pressed his palms against the napkin on his knee as he was introduced. Every eye turned his way as he stood. He fumbled with his notes as he approached the podium.

"Ladies and gentlemen, thank you for inviting me here tonight. . . ."

Tohni sighed and slumped against the kitchen wall. Thank goodness that part was over. Now all she had to do was wait until Reese was finished. She could hear his voice, growing in strength and enthusiasm. He sounded different. Curiously, she stood on tiptoe and peered through a window in the door between the kitchen and the banquet room. She stared at Reese.

It was definitely a different man who spoke so boldly to the rapt crowd of influential legislators. This Reese was extremely serious, knowledgeable, fervent. And what he was saying was

95

shocking. Tohni found herself hanging on to his words.

"Are we poisoning ourselves? Surely you're aware that there are risks as well as benefits from all the chemicals introduced into our environment. The federal government has the responsibility of permitting only those chemicals whose *benefits outweigh the risks.*" Reese paused for the proper audience response, then continued.

"Note the variance of toxic chemicals found in these water samples taken at regular intervals right out here in this lake fed by the Tennessee River. And the river is regularly monitored. But you can see the preponderance of chemicals in certain areas of the lake." He passed around the vials he'd collected and tested the day Tohni observed him from her fishing boat.

"You've all heard of Love Canal. But do you know about the Hardeman Dump Site, a west Tennessee farm that was turned into a chemical dump in the sixties without permits, licenses, or public announcements? In the ensuing years the inhabitants suffered documented illnesses and well-water contamination. There are others like this in California, Texas, Ohio, Arizona."

Tohni's eyes widened as Reese continued with a fervor she hadn't seen in all the time she'd observed him. As he rattled off the names of chemicals and their hazards to the environment, Tohni, grabbing a pencil, listed them on

96

her order pad. Reese held his audience—and Tohni—captive for almost an hour, making the usually dull subject of hazardous chemicals vital and interesting by citing examples of how certain chemicals affect everyone's life.

"The common term for illegal dumping of toxic-waste products is 'midnight dumping.' It is still occurring daily, nightly. In New Jersey. In Pennsylvania. In Oregon. Maybe in Tennessee."

He leaned on the podium. "Solutions are not simple. They require legislation, liability, enforcement, and the elimination of uncontrolled dumping sites. Who can we trust? How safe is safe? Who decides? Ladies and gentlemen, in the end, we do. We can no longer depend on industry to regulate itself, nor the government to protect us. It is a job we must do for ourselves."

Reese finished to a standing ovation. He'd made the impact he'd intended, accomplishing his goal for the present. Warnings had been given to the proper people. Now he had an even bigger goal, and it would take more documentation, proof rather than mere shocking statements like tonight's. It would take time, but he was determined to do it. Then what? Would he be ruined in the field of his choice? Or was he risking even greater danger? That of his own physical well-being?

The first one through the crowd was Tohni. She touched his arm. "Is all that stuff true, Reese honey?"

They were shoved together by the crowd. Her elbow dug into his midsection, her other arm pressed against his thigh. The intimacy was unavoidable, imposed on them by outside circumstances. She relished every moment of it.

"Of course it's true, Mandy."

She grinned admiringly. "Well, Mr. Thinker, this was lots more interesting than just garbage."

"More important too. Deadly."

"Reese, you were very good. . . ."

"Thanks, Mandy. Right now I need to talk to some of these legislators. They're influential and can make the crucial changes in the laws to tighten regulation of dump sites. Come over to my place in a couple of hours. Please."

As they were pushed apart she nodded, her gray eyes straining futilely to hold his blue gaze. Reese's attention was lost to a short, gray-haired man with intense eyes and a booming southern accent.

Oh, yes, she would meet him later. It was something she couldn't resist. Meantime maybe she could determine just who this man was. The same Reese Kreuger she'd been attracted to yesterday on the boat? The same Reese Kreuger she'd watched from hidden windows and treetops? Who was he anyway? And why did she care so much?

The crowd thinned out. The banquet room was restored to order. Reese had departed for private conferences with some of the legislators. Tohni was beat. Exhausted. She stood barefooted in the phone booth and dropped quarters until she got her long-distance connection.

"Joe? Got a pencil? Take these names down. Toluene. Dioxane. Methane. PCB. Check on them for me."

"Whoa! Hold it, Tohni. What is this?"

"They're chemicals, Joe. Just do it. Let me know. This guy's on to something."

"Who? Kreuger? You aren't getting too involved, are you, Tohni?"

"No, of course not." She rubbed her stockinged toes against her other leg.

"Good, because it's time to bring your man in. First thing tomorrow."

"What? No! Not yet, Joe!"

"What the hell, Tohni? You've been bugging me for days to end this. Do it tomorrow. That's what you're getting paid for."

"But, Joe—"

"Tohni, do you need any help bringing him in?" His tone was acerbic.

She licked her lips and blinked furiously. "Who, me? I don't have a black belt for nothing. Why, this guy'll be a piece of cake."

"Okay, kid. Listen closely. Someone'll meet you at the Executive Office Complex near the Loop, just north of the city. Twelve o'clock sharp. See you tomorrow."

"See ya, Joe."

"Oh, Tohni. Good job!"

99

"Yeah. Thanks." Stunned, Tohni replaced the phone. Tomorrow it would all be over. Tomorrow. All she and Reese had left was tonight.

In another part of Atlanta a phone rang. A man's hand, sporting a six-carat, square-cut diamond set in a solid-gold band, lifted the receiver.

"Yes?"

"Cornell, they've got him."

"The hell you say." He chuckled low in his throat. "Where?"

"Somewhere up in Tennessee. Around Chattanooga, I think. They're bringing him in tomorrow."

"Hell, it's about time."

"I'm having someone meet them at Executive Office Plaza, out near the Loop. Don't want to take any chances on him getting away."

"Good thinking, Jacoby."

"Should we . . . bring him to you first?"

There was a pause, then Cornell said, "Sure. We'll give him one more chance. Why not? If he's still stubborn, you'll know what to do."

"Yessir."

A single small lamp cast a shadow behind the tall man who slipped quietly into the cabin on the lake.

"Is this a cat burglar or a cuddly kitten curled

up on my sofa?" he murmured in a gravelly voice.

Tohni awoke with a start, then smiled at the handsome face nuzzling her ear. "Hi. I must have fallen asleep waiting for you. What time is it?"

"After one. How did you get in? The place was locked."

She stretched lazily, arching her breasts outward as her arms reached up. "Don't ask a country girl all her secrets."

It was with considerable restraint that he kept his hands off her inviting little body. "Would you like a nightcap?"

"What are you offering?"

He thought for a minute. "Ward brought over some applejack. Would you like it warmed with a stick of cinnamon?"

Tohni smiled. "I'd love it." She got up and padded barefooted after Reese into the small kitchen. "What have you been doing all this time?"

Tohni had gone home, showered, changed clothes, packed, and slid her resignation under the Catfish King's door. Breaking into Reese's cabin had been simple; the waiting had been tough. She fell asleep arguing with herself over what to tell him, and how. Now that he was here she couldn't bring herself to admit the truth. At least not yet.

"I've been talking to people who make the laws in this state and others on committees in Congress involved with environmental issues.

101

Tonight was very important for my latest project. Time got away from me though. When I realized how late it was I thought you might not come." He poured the golden liquid into a pan and set it on the gas stove. "I'm glad you did."

Tohni folded her arms and watched him. It was still the most pleasurable part of her job. During these moments, as he made himself comfortable and began to unwind, she wondered exactly why she had agreed to come tonight. She was far too attracted to him for her own good. And far too willing!

Under her scrutiny Reese removed his suit jacket and loosened his tie. The golden tan of his skin contrasted with the stark white of his dress shirt. Suddenly, she felt a dangerous desire; she wanted to see more of that golden skin.

Reese looked at her expectantly. "I wanted you to come here tonight so we could talk, Mandy."

"I want to talk too, Reese honey." Tohni smiled, deciding to hide behind Mandy's boldness. "I want to tell you how proud I was of you tonight. You really know a lot about important stuff, like those chemicals."

Reese smiled tightly and took her hand. Before she realized what he was doing, he'd pressed the palm to his lips. She gasped at his touch, which sent hot, exciting sensations coursing through her.

"Thanks, Mandy." He smiled gently. "You

don't know how much it means to me to have you behind me. That's why I wanted you to be there tonight. And why I must tell you what I'm doing."

She felt her body grow tense and longed for the strength of his arms. A closeness, a warm sensuous veil settled over them, something inside Tohni snapped. Nothing mattered but the two of them. Not her job. Not his. Not tomorrow. Only tonight.

She fought those mounting feelings and cleared her throat. "What are you talking about, Reese honey? You seem so serious." She tugged her hand from his.

"Did you understand what I was talking about tonight, Mandy? How important it is for everyone to be concerned about toxic waste?"

She grinned proudly. "Why, Reese honey, you had those city slickers in the palm of your hand. And me too. That's real important stuff. I always knew you were a serious thinker, but I had no idea how deep you went. You must be real smart."

"Mandy, that 'stuff,' as you call it, is very important to me. It's my work. At times it's almost an obsession. The deeper you get, the more you find out." He reached out and let a single finger trail along her cheek. He lifted her chin. His lips were alarmingly close to hers, yet he refrained from the inevitable kiss. "In a way, it's like you, Mandy. Except the more I know about you, the more I like what I find."

"You, uh, don't really know much about me,

103

Reese. And you might not like what you find if you dig too deep." She tried to back away, but he caught both of her hands and placed them at his waist.

"You aren't married, are you?" His voice was a low growl.

She swallowed hard. "Oh, heavens, no! It's just that I, uh, we're so different. Why, I haven't even heard of most of those chemicals you mentioned tonight."

"You aren't the only one, Mandy. Most people haven't. That's the problem. But somebody's got to speak out. People are watching me. In fact, I probably took a risk tonight by making a public speech. But it's something I felt I had to do."

"Wh-what people are watching you?" She grew instantly hot. Could he possibly know that she was the one?

"People who don't want me to speak out the way I did tonight."

"But, Reese honey, it sounds so important. I admire a man with convictions." She laughed nervously. "And all this time I thought you were staying out here by the lake for a little fishing vacation. But you've been busy sampling the water around here and doing all kinds of important things that I don't understand."

"I want to explain it so you will understand what I'm doing."

"And I want to know," she agreed eagerly, trying to pull out of his close embrace.

"Just relax, Mandy," he urged. "I won't hurt you."

Relax? He must be crazy! Tohni's eyes darted frantically to the stove, where the pan was steaming vigorously. "Reese! The applejack is boiling over!"

They tore apart and Reese scooted to lift the pan from the hot range, spilling a small amber puddle on the stove. "Damn!" he muttered beneath his breath.

"That's okay, Reese honey. I'll help you clean it up." Tohni grabbed a dishtowel and mopped the hot liquid.

Reese poured two mugs of spicy apple cider and handed her one. "Why don't we go sit down where we can relax?"

Tohni was grateful for the diversion of the cider. And they had something else to think of besides themselves. "You were telling me about your job." She quickly slipped out of the tiny kitchen, determined to stay out his arms. It was difficult to think straight while inhaling his spellbinding fragrance.

Before she could dart to the chair, he clasped her hand and steered her to the sofa. "Mandy, I'm glad you understand the importance of my work . . ."

She nodded enthusiastically. "Oh, I do. I do."

He looked at her curiously and finished his sentence. ". . . to everyone."

She lowered her head and sipped at the cider. He watched her for a moment, then raised his steamy cup to his lips. The air was redolent with the spicy smell, and it brought a smile to Tohni's lips. "This reminds me of childhood. Candy apples and cotton candy. It's very good."

He nodded, his dark eyes hooded as he slouched beside her on the sofa. "I'll tell Ward we enjoyed it."

Tohni's gaze swept over his lean, relaxed form and she murmured softly, "Reese honey, it's getting late and you're tired. Why don't we finish this conversation tomorrow?"

"Yes, it can wait. Everything can but us, Mandy. Only one thing is important to me now," he whispered, and drew her closer, pressing her to his broad chest. "You and me."

"Reese . . . Reese, wait. We've got to talk about this."

"I think we've talked enough for one night."

"Reese honey, you haven't told me about—"

"I'll tell you later." One arm encircled her shoulders while his other hand lifted her face to his. Slowly, mesmerizingly, his lips lowered to hers. The sweet touch was like a firebrand, setting off a tempest within her. She didn't—couldn't—fight his kiss, but was content to let the wildfire engulf them both. Simmering passion sprang to sizzling life as lips and tongues played against each other.

When he finally broke away, she was breathless. So was he. "Mandy, my sweet, sweet Mandy. Tell me you didn't feel that kiss all the way—"

She squirmed. "Well, of course I felt it, Reese honey. I'd have to be frozen not to."

His grin was devilish. "And we both know you aren't frozen." His fingers dug into the knot of his tie, undid it, and let it hang free. He unbuttoned two buttons of his stiff white shirt, and then her hands closed over his.

She tried not to notice the golden skin beneath the open collar. "Reese honey, listen to me. You probably won't be here much longer. And I can assure you I do not intend to—"

He kissed her again, this time drawing her into an even more passionate embrace. Her head spun with the intoxicating strength of his kiss, the teasing of his tongue against her lips. It was with a great deal of difficulty and fortitude that she pushed herself to her feet. "Reese, I can't let this go on. You see, there are things about me you don't know."

"What do you mean by that?" He stood up beside her.

"I . . ." She thought frantically. There had been enough lies between them. Maybe it was time for truth. "Reese, I've been after you all along."

"I've been after you too, Mandy," he murmured with a soft chuckle, drawing her into the warm shelter of his arms. "Looks like we caught each other."

Wordlessly, without further coaxing, she was in his arms, reaching tentatively for his shoulders, then slipping her fingers into the silken path of hair at the back of his neck. She lifted her gray eyes to meet his, fierce desire in his expression. Then as their lips merged again, she closed her eyes and allowed her desire to soar with his.

His kisses left her weak, his hands caressing her breasts until they were throbbing points of fire. He squeezed the tips gently, then pressed his hard, masculine planes to her softer feminine curves. They fitted together nicely. And the heat between them was unmistakable.

"I want you, Mandy. Only one thing will satisfy this longing. Surely you feel it too."

Her gray eyes were dark with passion. "I feel everything you do," she whispered. "You make this so difficult, Reese." How could she tell him the truth now?

"Say yes, Mandy. Let me make love to you. Tonight."

She took a deep, trembling breath. *Reese, darling, we only have tonight!* she wanted to exclaim. She nodded and her dark hair fluffed around her pale face, emphasizing her large eyes. "Tonight is all that matters to me, Reese."

"Are you saying yes?"

She nodded again and whispered, "Yes, make love to me, Reese."

Slowly he began to remove her clothes, right there in the living room. First her blouse, then the lacy bra that hid her breasts. He breathed deeply at the sight of her.

His eyes never left her, unable—no, unwilling—to turn away. He focused on the glorious creamy mounds, then on her smiling, satisfied face, then again on her slender body.

Deftly, he unsnapped her jeans, easing them along with her panties off her gently rounded hips. She stepped from the pile of rumpled clothes and stood before him. Completely nude. And beautiful.

He placed his right hand over her left breast. His large, rough palm centered on the aroused nipple, the long fingers spread to enclose the entire swollen circle.

His other hand went to her back, pressing and stroking her silken skin. "Mandy, you're so perfect."

"Oh, Reese . . ."

"You're so beautiful, I want to feast on every inch of you." His lips moved to a nipple and closed over it.

She trembled in response and placed her hands on his shoulders. "I love it when you do that," she moaned. A rush of warmth flooded her with sensations too overwhelming to ignore. She almost crumpled to the floor in her passion-weakened state. She wanted to have him touch her all over, to welcome him into every cell of her body, to feel him inside her.

His eager kisses left moist trails over her body, until she ached with longing. His hands and lips caressed her everywhere, brushing, prodding, invading. Just before she reached the crest of desire he stopped, leaving her to quiver and throb with need.

"Wait for me, little vixen," he murmured, tickling her nipples again with his tongue.

"Reese, don't stop now."

So he sought the part of her she most wanted him to touch. She whimpered softly and pushed herself hard against him. Then, without another word, he swung her up in his arms and walked swiftly to the bedroom. While he peeled off his clothes she writhed on the bed with a dull aching she'd never before experienced. Her body throbbed with unsatisfied longing. When he joined her, the hot length of his passion brushed her thigh. Unable to hold back, he forged his way to her feminine sweetness.

With a small cry she eagerly accepted him, running her hands along his sinewy back down to the curve of his buttocks.

Once inside her, he held very still, relishing the moment, trying to slow things down. He knew, from the growing volcano inside him, this calm would only last a brief time before he exploded into her. "Mandy, are you all right? Am I hurting you?"

She tightened around him. She, too, savored the moment of possession. All too soon he would be gone and she would be empty. "I'm fine. Don't stop now. I want all of you, Reese."

"Mandy, oh, God, you set me on fire," he whispered huskily.

He hesitated a moment longer, then moved within her, with her, in a growing rampage of passionate fury. His strength almost lifted her

110

off the bed, but she met his power with her own strong thrusts. On and on they drove, oblivious to everything but their fierce desire for each other. The fire grew in them, blazing higher and higher until it set off a wild explosion that seized them both and sent them soaring in a white-hot frenzy.

Tohni cried aloud. She startled herself with her own voice, for it sounded almost animal-like. It was something she had never done before. Nor had she ever experienced such overwhelming passion. And she wanted the moment, the entire experience, to last forever.

"Mandy," he muttered, then again, louder, "Mandy."

"Hmm?"

"Mandy, are you all right?"

"I'm asleep. My wildest dream just came true."

He chuckled and kissed her tenderly. She clasped his head and pulled it to her, kissing him with fevered lips. "Reese, I've never felt like this before. Never. Don't leave me."

He returned her kiss. "I'm right here. All night."

"Come on, Reese honey. Let's do it again." She wriggled seductively beneath him.

He nuzzled her neck affectionately. "Give me time, you little tease. Give me time."

In the morning Tohni was the first to awaken. She slipped out of bed and took a shower. Leaving Reese to sleep, she roamed

111

out to the kitchen and made coffee. She had some thinking to do. How could she turn him in after last night? No matter what he had done, she didn't want to be the one to bring him in. But looming heavy and black was the question: Why had she weakened and gone to bed with him last night?

She sighed. The answer was simple. She was just a woman, and a vulnerable one at that. And Reese Kreuger was a damned handsome man. An appealing man whose intelligence and honesty intrigued her. She'd become caught up in something beyond her control. It wasn't an answer she could give Joe, but it was one she could live with.

She was finishing her first cup of coffee when Reese came sleepily to the doorway. He was nude, golden, and absolutely gorgeous. And then she knew for certain why she'd broken her own rules and made love with him. She cared more about this man than she feared the consequences of the night. That, too, was not a reason she could give Joe. But it was one she tucked away in her heart.

"Mornin'," she said, admiring his sleek body in the gray light. Oh, God, had they really made love all night? How she wanted to rush to him now, wrap her arms around him, tell him how she felt. But she couldn't. There wasn't time. They were already late.

"Been up long?"

She shook her head. "Just long enough to take a shower."

"Sounds like a winner."

"Want some coffee first? It's ready."

He turned away. "No, I think I'll chase the bears away first."

Tohni drank another cup of coffee while she waited. It was a period of dread, like waiting for a hurricane to hit. You know it's coming, a vicious force you've never experienced before. You know it might destroy everything you've worked so hard to build. You know things will never be the same again. But finally you just want it to come, so you can get over and be done with it. She felt that way now.

She could hear the shower running, the water no doubt pelting his broad shoulders and muscular chest. He would be lathering the lean, masculine planes of his body, letting the pulsing stream rinse him clean. Oh, God, how she wanted to touch him. Everywhere. Just touch him again. But she didn't dare.

The shower stopped.

She paced across the room, then forced herself to sit again, feigning a calmness she certainly didn't feel.

He appeared in the doorway, this time in jeans and a blue sport shirt. He'd combed his thick sandy hair back and it lay in damp strands. He was so damned handsome.

Reese bent to the window and squinted at the foggy morning. "It's awfully dark. What time is it?"

"It's getting late. Ten-thirty. We've got cloud

113

cover. Probably going to rain." So much for the weather, she thought nervously.

"Late for what?" Reese poured himself a cup of coffee, then came toward her. She looked strange. Strained. Maybe she was already regretting what had happened last night. "Are you all right, Mandy?" He touched her cheek gently with the back of his hand.

She jerked away, unable to deal with the upheaval inside her. Unable to bear his touch when she was about to betray him. Her voice was raspy. "Late for our trip to Atlanta."

"What trip?" He looked at her curiously, gulped the coffee, and repeated, "What trip to Atlanta? I don't remember making plans to that effect, Mandy."

She sighed and stood. It always made her feel more in control when she stood because she was so short. Right now she wished she were ten feet tall and hated Reese Kreuger. But neither was true. Tohni's eyes were large and sad as she spoke in a rather shaky voice. There was nothing cool and detached about her today. Tohni York, private investigator, was an absolute wreck.

The words came in a rush. "Reese, there's something I have to tell you. I'm not Mandy Johnson. I'm Tohni York, an operative for Eagle Eye Investigations of Atlanta. I was hired by the Ansel Corporation to bring you in."

CHAPTER SEVEN

"You're a what?" Reese said angrily.

"I work for an investigation firm in Atlanta. I'm a—"

"Private eye? Oh, hell!" Reese's face darkened with rage and betrayal. "I don't believe it!"

"It's true." She showed him a little plastic card complete with photo, identifying her as Agent 201, officially licensed.

He looked at the card, then at her. "I'll be damned. What a fool I've been." His eyes cut into her and his lips curled in a derisive grin. "You deceitful little witch."

Tohni felt very small indeed, but she had to try to explain what she'd done. "I hired on at the Catfish King to keep an eye on you. I know you jog every morning at six. I watched you the day you went out with Ward Sutton and gathered water samples. Remember the old fisherman in the boat who kept catching fish? That was me. I've reported on you every day for the last two weeks."

He glowered darkly at her as the reality of

what she was saying began to dawn on him. "Will you also make a report on last night, detailing how many times we made love?"

She felt a hot rush of adrenaline, of guilt. "I know what you're thinking, Reese, but last night I could only think of losing you. And I didn't want that to happen."

"Like hell! You didn't want me out of your sight! What better way to keep an eye on me than to spend the night with me?"

"That's not so. I knew that last night would be our last for a while and I just lost—"

His lips drew back in a vicious scowl. "Correction, *honey*. That was our first and last time *ever!* Once can be chalked up as a mistake, but to go back to the same foul waters would make me a fool for sure."

"Reese, please let me explain."

"Explain why you deceived me? Why you've been spying on me for days? Yeah, sure. I'm dying to hear your side of it."

She pressed her hands together nervously. This was harder than she'd dreamed it would be. "Reese, I want you to know that I care very much about you. And about what you're doing with your toxic-waste projects. I know it's an extremely important issue. But you must realize I have a job to do too. That's how I got involved in this in the first place. I was assigned to find someone. It was strictly routine—until now."

"You care about my work? About me? That's

116

a laugh! You have a funny way of showing how you care for somebody. Spying!"

"Do you realize that I've never been so close, so concerned about a subject?"

"Never gone to bed with one? Aw, come on, Mandy. You seemed so skilled at it!"

"No! Never! I . . . I could lose my job over this. Over last night."

He laughed scornfully. "And I'm supposed to believe that? I could swear you were hired to do what you did! And I must admit, you're very good at it. There's a name for women like you."

Her eyes smarted with the pain of his blunt accusation. "I'm telling you the truth, Reese."

"After what you've just revealed, how do you expect me to believe anything you say? The trust between us has just been destroyed. You killed it. I can't believe anything you say."

"I'm sorry, Reese. Maybe later we can change all this."

"Don't bank on it, Mandy."

"My name's Tohni York. And you can believe that all I expect you to do is accompany me back to Atlanta today. Ansel only wants to talk to you. That's all."

"You're getting involved in something you don't know anything about. You don't really know what Ansel wants with me. He is an evil, vindictive man."

She shrugged. "At first I thought it might have something to do with your divorce. Alimony or something. That's the usual reason for hiring a private service to find someone. Now, though, I figure it's about the business."

"Oh, it's about the business all right. Big Daddy and I clashed on almost every company policy."

"Apparently he's changed his mind." She gave him a hopeful look.

Reese shook his head. He stalked over to pour more coffee into his mug. "No, he hasn't changed his mind, Mandy."

"Tohni."

"Tohni! Whatever your name is!" He gestured angrily in the air. "Ansel wants me to shut my mouth about the company's midnight dumps. You know what that is. Illegal dumping. And the facts are, I know too much about them and Ansel wants to make sure I keep quiet. Worse yet, I've already contacted the EPA. They're on to Ansel's practices. The trick is to document past transgressions or catch them in the act. That's where I come in. I can document illegal dumping during the last three years because I was in on it."

"Reese, all that can be settled with them now. Ansel said to tell you he's ready to negotiate."

"Negotiate? Yeah. On his terms."

She spread her palms before him. "Maybe he sees he can't continue these illegal practices. He's ready to change and wants your cooperation."

"That's utterly ridiculous! Does the leopard

118

change his spots when he's caged? You don't know the man at all. He's vicious."

"It isn't my job to know or question the integrity of the people who hire me. Nor is it my job to check with my subject on his or her opinion of the situation. I've already overstepped my bounds with you, Reese."

"You mean over*slept*, don't you?"

She looked down at her toes. "I could get fired for such behavior. We . . . I . . . went too far."

He gulped his coffee and set the mug down with a clatter. "Well, sweetie, you might be in deep trouble, but I don't give a damn. I'd love to be the one to tell your boss how eagerly you went to bed with me. And what a hot little number you were. However, it just doesn't fit into my schedule. I'm afraid Atlanta is a little out of my way right now. I definitely won't be going back with you."

"Reese, don't make this more difficult than it already is. For both of us." But how could she expect him to believe how much she was hurting inside right now?

"Difficult?" he said. "How about impossible! You've made a fool of me once, Mandy—er, Tohni. It won't happen again. I'm walking out of here. Without you."

"Don't do it, Reese."

"Just what would you do if I started out that door?" He sneered. "I am bigger than you, you know."

"I'd stop you, Reese. It's my job."

119

"Well, Tohni York, little Miss Private Eye, do your job!" He started for the back door.

Swiftly, with moves as sure and smooth as an ancient warrior's, Tohni reacted.

Facing Reese, she slid her right knee between his legs. As he came forward with his next natural step, she tripped him over her leg and swung him hard to the floor. His own weight carried him down with a resounding thud. Immediately, she knelt on one knee and brought his right arm up behind his back. Reese was pinned. And stunned. She had used the oldest trick in the book, the element of surprise. And it worked!

Tohni stared at the large prone form beneath her knee, and only then realized what she'd done. It had been an integral part of her training; a reflex action threw her into motion when she saw her subject escaping.

Subject? What in hell was wrong with her? Why, this was Reese!

Immediately, she straightened his arm and turned him over on his back. Tenderly, she cradled his head. A small red bump in the middle of his forehead indicated how hard he'd hit the floor.

"Reese honey, I'm sorry. Did I hurt you?" Her hands framed his face and pressed it to her bosom. She kissed the bump, and both of his tanned cheeks. "Reese? Oh, God, Reese! Please speak to me."

As if in response to her plea he groaned and began to thrash around.

"Reese, are you all right?"

He opened his blue eyes and looked into her hovering face. "Damn! For a little pip-squeak, you really pack a wallop."

"Does it hurt? Oh, Reese!"

"When you go after a guy, you don't stop short of knocking him flat. Why didn't you just say 'If you take another step, I'm gonna knock hell outta you'?"

She grinned. "Because you wouldn't have believed me."

"You're right," he muttered cynically. "You've made me a believer now."

"Reese, I'm really sorry. I didn't mean for you to fall so hard. I . . . I guess I caught you off-guard. I certainly didn't mean to hurt you."

"I'll bet you say that to all the guys," he said with scorn, struggling to a sitting position.

"Actually, this is the first time I've ever hit anyone hard enough to stun him."

He cast her a contemptuous glance. "I'm up for all kinds of firsts, aren't I?"

She tried to ignore his disdain, leaning close. "Let me look at your eyes. If your pupils are uneven, that's not good."

"If I'm left alone in the room with you, that's not good. You're a dangerous little woman, Mandy."

"Tohni."

He rolled his eyes and sighed. "Whoever."

"Reese, I don't know what happened to me just then. It all happened so fast. One minute we were talking. The next, I saw you leaving.

121

And I could think of only one thing. To stop you."

"Good training," he groaned. "Remind me to add that to your list of attributes when I talk to your boss."

"Reese . . . I'm sorry."

"So am I."

"I mean about everything."

"Me too. Things were going pretty good between us for a while. But some things are hard to overlook. Like lying. And knocking the hell outta your lover. Not exactly romantic, you know!"

"I know." She looked down at her hands. "I ruined it. And honest to God, I didn't mean to. You're the best—oh, hell."

"The best lay?" he spat out.

"Reese!" Her large gray eyes filled with unwelcome tears and she dashed them away. "Please don't say that. You know I didn't feel that way about it. About us. I tried to keep it purely on a business level."

"And now you're going to say it's my fault."

She sniffed. "No. It's mine. I was wrong to . . . give in to lust. But I don't regret what we shared."

"Don't give me that line!" he said sardonically. "Surely you aren't thinking I'll go along with your crazy schemes and we'll somehow end up where we broke off last night! Come on, Mandy—I mean Tohni! It's over!"

"I guess it was an unrealistic hope," she said weakly. "But I still expect you to accompany me to Atlanta. I think you've got to try to patch things up with Ansel. You can't stay on the run forever."

He bit his lower lip for a moment. "Maybe you're right. Now is the time to end this. Tell you what. To keep you from hog-tying me and tossing me in the back of your car, I'll go with you. I'll go find out what Ansel's got on his mind, and let him know what's on mine. We haven't talked face to face in several months. Maybe he has had a change of heart."

"You'll go? Oh, Reese, that's great." She had begun to worry that she'd have some fast explaining to do to Joe if Reese stood firm in refusing to go with her, or if he somehow gave her the slip. And worse yet would be explaining it to Ansel. "This . . . you'll make it much smoother for both of us. Now all this can be settled. And you can get on with your business."

"And you get to keep your job. Don't thank me now, please. If we shake hands, you might decide to flip me over your shoulder." He stood up. "Only one thing. Give me time to gather my material. I need to take all my papers and reports. It'll take a while to get them organized, since I hadn't planned on leaving yet."

"Of course." She nodded. "I'll help you pack."

In a rather strained silence the two worked together. Reese threw his clothes into a suitcase, his papers into a fat brown briefcase. Tohni stacked folders and papers. Reese put them in order and loaded the car. It was nearly noon and raining steadily when they pulled away from the lakeside cabin. One brief stop at Tohni's apartment to pick up her suitcase and they were on their way.

"You hungry?"

He shrugged. "Last supper before the Judas kiss?"

She tightened her lips. He was bitter. She couldn't blame him. She had betrayed him.

She pulled off the highway at the red-and-white sign of a fast-food restaurant. "Fried chicken sound okay?"

A muscle in his jaw quivered. He refused to look at her. "Do you trust me to go in? Or shall I slip into the handcuffs first?"

"Damn it, Reese. Of course I trust—" Her voice broke. It was worse than anything he could say to her: There wasn't a shred of trust in his eyes anymore.

She fumbled in her purse, but before she could draw out any money he opened the door. "My treat," he said with a sneer, and dashed through the pouring rain.

Since they were already behind schedule, Tohni didn't want to take time out to eat. So they crunched chicken legs in transit. Very few words were spoken as they flew down the highway from Chattanooga toward Atlanta.

Reese wiped his hands on a moist towel the restaurant had provided and stuffed the remnants of their lunch into the paper bag. He watched the countryside with feigned interest

124

as they drove deeper in to the familiar red-clay country around Atlanta.

He glanced at the petite woman beside him. Who was she anyway? He'd eagerly accepted her as the gum-popping waitress Mandy Johnson, grateful for her earthy view of life and love. She'd been a welcome relief from the pressures and boredom of the last few months. She had pretended to be a woman who didn't care for status or money, only for the delights of her simple life. And he'd believed her.

God, what a fool he'd been. She wasn't that kind of woman at all. She was a woman doing her job. A woman who could fight. And lie. And deceive without the bat of an eye. And he'd fallen for her act, not even considering the possibility of what she might be doing. But then he never dreamed that Ansel was actually serious enough to hire someone to find him. Oh, she was a scheming little witch all right.

Well, he could scheme too. He'd told Mandy . . . er, Tohni, that he'd go with her to Atlanta. But he'd only go to face Ansel on his own terms. With a lawyer. With documented evidence in hand. He could easily elude Tohni once they arrived in town. The fact that she'd managed to catch him off-balance and off-guard once only meant he'd be more alert the next time. He knew now he couldn't trust her for a minute. Well, she couldn't trust him either. Only she didn't know it yet.

He glanced at her again. What kind of woman would have such a dirty job? What kind could go to bed with a man, then betray him? He sighed and leaned back on the headrest. Closing his eyes, he decided she'd have to be a pretty devious female to do what she'd done. Did she know that if he allowed her to take him all the way to Ansel's, it might bring about his demise?

Tohni was somewhat relieved to notice that Reese could nap at a time like this. Her mind whirled at the same pace as the fleeting pine trees outside the car windows. Instead of feeling satisfied with a mission almost accomplished, she felt uneasy and fitful. There were strong antagonistic vibes in the car, and perhaps she deserved them. The two were now bitter enemies, on opposite sides of the fence.

She should've felt relieved that it was almost over, yet she felt anxious. She knew she was the betrayer Reese accused her of being.

Tohni glanced at her watch. Two o'clock. They were very late. She should have phoned to tell Joe they were off schedule. What if the people who were supposed to meet them had left?

At the junction with the 285 Loop, she turned off Interstate 75 and pulled into the parking lot of the Executive Office Complex where her assignment was supposed to be concluded. Immediately, a black limousine pulled up alongside the passenger side of her car. The door opened, then Reese's door was opened and two huge men dressed in three-piece suits grabbed Reese. They didn't say a word as they jerked him from his seat.

"What the hell—" he exclaimed, and tried to push them away. "Get your hands off me!"

One man held his right arm firmly, but he slipped the other arm free and swung wildly at the other thug, who was moving in to restrain him.

Tohni stared open-mouthed, then stammered, "Hey, not so rough, you jerks!"

For someone who usually reacted quickly, she was momentarily stunned. This was definitely not the reception she'd expected. These men certainly weren't acting like legitimate businessmen, but maybe it was his fault. Maybe he hadn't told her everything. Maybe everything he'd told her wasn't true.

Another large man joined the two ruffians in restraining Reese. He was caught! He cast a glance at Tohni and there was no mistaking his contempt. She had tricked him and now there was no way out. She cringed beneath his gaze as one of the men slammed her car door shut.

They hustled Reese into the other vehicle.

"Wait a minute. You forgot his luggage!" Tohni looked at the two suitcases abandoned in the backseat, then at the black limo moving rapidly out of the parking lot. Reese had carefully packed the briefcase. It was important to him. But they hadn't wanted the briefcase. Only Reese. Maybe they just forgot. No, she had the bone-chilling feeling they knew exactly what they were doing.

127

They had forced Reese to go with them. Effectively abducted him! And she had engineered it! What the hell was going on here? She had to talk to Joe about this right away.

Tohni gripped the steering wheel and laid her forehead on her hands. She didn't want to believe what she'd just seen. And she knew what Joe would tell her. "You did your part. Don't worry about the rest." But she couldn't help it. Because it involved Reese. And she cared. Oh, she cared too damn much!

She needed to forget Reese Kreuger. She needed to forget her inexcusably unprofessional behavior, forget the awkward affair she'd had with a subject—a subject whose beautiful tanned face wouldn't leave her memory. It seemed impossible to forget, but she had to. It was part of her job. And anyway what could she do? Go to the police? Joe would have her head.

But she needed help. There was one person in Georgia who could help her at a time like this. She pressed her foot to the accelerator and headed for Decatur.

The door to the elegant Georgian house swung open. "Tohni! What a wonderful surprise!"

"Mama? How about if I take you out for dinner tonight?"

"Nonsense! You come in this house this instant. What you need is a good home-cooked meal!"

Tohni let herself be whisked into the spotless house to be hugged by her mother, Vera Lee, and Stella, her mother's longtime maid. The two women hovered around her like honeybees to a gardenia, and Tohni tried to appreciate their praise and attention. Soon she found herself sitting on the back veranda, sipping a mint julep beneath a flowering magnolia tree. Yes, this was what she needed. Mama's touch. But she wondered what Mama would say if she knew her own daughter was a liar and a traitor!

Vera Lee rambled on about her newest bridge partner and her latest blue ribbon at the annual flower show. Ordinarily Tohni loved it. She leaned back and tried to take delight in her mother's entertainment. Vera Lee was everything Tohni was not. First and foremost, Vera Lee was a proper southern lady. She behaved in the appropriate manner, married the right men, was the perfect housewife and the almost-perfect mother. The fact that Vera Lee had outlived three husbands by the time she was fifty-three was a source of amazement—and amusement—to Tohni.

Well, it wasn't exactly funny of course. Just ironic that by playing the society game just right, Vera Lee had managed to move up in life and now lived in a lovely Georgian home in a wealthy section of Atlanta, all because she married the right men. But never, *never* would she consider consorting with a gentleman outside the bonds of matrimony.

Tohni's father had died when she was only

three. Vera Lee was left a beautiful blond widow with a darling little dark-haired girl . . . for about a year. Then she married the physician who'd treated her fatally ill husband.

Dr. Woodrow Wynn was a dedicated man who worked long hours and brought home an amazing amount of money. They lived in a fine house with a swimming pool, and he sent Tohni to the finest private schools in Atlanta. However, the good doctor died young, leaving Vera Lee a widow again.

A year later Vera Lee married a lawyer. By then Tohni was finishing high school and heading for college. Her main concern was that the new husband treat her mother well.

Her worries were quickly dispelled. Thurlow Stanfield treated Vera Lee like a queen. He showered her with gifts, flowers, and trips around the world. Vera Lee was the happiest she'd ever been, and Tohni felt she probably loved Thurlow more than any of the others.

A little over a year ago Thurlow had dropped dead of a heart attack. No warning. It was quite tragic. Vera Lee had been disconsolate for months. Only Stella could reach her.

Tohni looked at her mother now as she chatted amiably. Vera Lee had been alone for more than a year now, and Tohni was glad to see a light again in her mother's eyes. Life had been so unfair to Vera Lee. She'd had more than her share of grief. Yet she could still hold her head up and laugh and Tohni admired her tremendously, and loved her dearly.

After dinner they lingered over coffee. Vera Lee traced the china cup's paper-thin rim. "Tohni, what's wrong? You hardly ate anything tonight."

"I just wasn't very hungry, Mama."

"Nonsense. Fried chicken is one of your favorites. And Stella fixes it better than anybody."

How could she tell her mother that fried chicken reminded her so much of Reese that she couldn't stand it. Where was he tonight? What was he eating?

Vera Lee subjected her to closer scrutiny. "You look like you've lost a little weight since I last saw you, sugar."

"I've been busy, Mama. Just got back from a job up at Chickamauga in Tennessee."

Vera Lee shook her finger at her daughter. "That's what it is! That crazy job, Tohni. When are you going to give it up and do something normal? Why, you could go back and finish law school."

"I don't want to finish law school, Mama. There isn't anything wrong with my work. Anyway, I happen to like it."

"Spying on people?" Vera Lee leaned back and sighed. "I never thought I'd see the day when my own daughter would resort to hiding in abandoned buildings, spying on people with binoculars."

"Don't forget climbing trees," Tohni quipped.

131

"And dressing up in all those crazy disguises."

"I've been a waitress for the past two weeks," Tohni mused. "You should have seen me!"

"Well, it's certainly not like you. Not the real you, Tohni." Vera Lee gave her daughter an accusing glare and folded her arms primly.

Tohni blinked and looked curiously at her mother for a moment. How could her mother thrust right to the heart of the matter without knowing a thing about Tohni's trouble? Until today, she had been content to dress up as other people, play her games, and do her unusual job. Until today, it had been the perfect job. Now, suddenly, she hated it. And herself.

Irritably, she snapped, "It isn't the job, Mama. Everything's fine."

Vera Lee's lovely blue eyes softened and she leaned forward, touching her daughter's hand. "Something's wrong with you. I can tell. I know you too well, sugar. Is it a man?"

"A man? Ha!" Tohni's scoff was too quick, too loud. "You think everything revolves around men, Mama!"

Vera Lee folded her arms and gave her daughter a solemn look. "You can deny it all you want to, Tohni. But you must admit I know about these things. I've had lots of experience for a woman of my station in life. You have a funny, miserable look in your eyes. You aren't in love, are you, sugar?"

Tohni's breath caught in her throat, forcing a

132

soft cough. Then she said in a spurt, "Me? In love? Of course not! Don't be silly!" *How can I be in love with a man I've lied to and betrayed? A man who hates mé!*

Vera Lee didn't reply, but just sat looking steadily at her daughter's distraught face. She knew love when she saw it. Many times it had a lot to do with misery.

CHAPTER EIGHT

"Joe, I'm telling you there was something fishy about the way they met us. They were not your regular corporate execs. They were too rude and hostile."

"Don't read more into it than you should, Tohni."

She paced around the small office from which Eagle Eye operated, her fury increasing along with the decibel level of her voice. "First, I think the men were somebody's goons. Even though they were dressed in three-piece suits, they were huge giants and rough as hell. They completely ignored me. And without a word of introduction or identification, they grabbed Reese and shoved him into that big black car. It was almost like an abduction! A kidnapping! Oh, God, Joe, maybe it was a kidnapping!"

Joe Staci, a man of about fifty, sat patiently for a moment, listening to Tohni's account of the events. His dark brown eyes steadily assessed her, and his ruddy face wore an expression of tolerance.

"Tohni, anybody over five-six looks like a giant to you. Now I've been in this business a long time and I've seen just about everything. This isn't so unusual. Ansel's people paid us to find Reese Kreuger. They wanted him real bad because he'd been eluding them for weeks. So when they saw him, they grabbed him quick. That's all." He shrugged hefty shoulders and turned back to the paperwork on his desk.

"What if it wasn't even Ansel's people who took Reese?"

"They were Ansel's. If not, I would have heard from them by now."

"But, Joe, if they wanted him so badly just to negotiate new company policies, why did they leave his suitcase in my car? And his briefcase? Especially his briefcase, which contained all his important papers."

"Maybe they just forgot about them." Joe kept his gray head bent over his work, trying to ignore her.

"Unless they didn't know about the briefcase," Tohni said, reasoning aloud. "Or didn't care."

"Hmm, maybe. Just hang on to everything until they call. He'll need his clothes in a day or two. Stick them in the storage cabinet until they call." He motioned to the cabinet in the hall.

"I'll hang on to them all right," Tohni murmured, thinking of where she'd stuffed them, in the back of a closet in her own apartment.

"Or you could just give Ansel's office a call

and tell them what you have. Get the stuff out of our way."

"Oh, no, Joe. That might be dangerous. If they don't know about Reese's papers, why turn them over to the wrong people? They belong to Reese. And he's the one who should get them back, not Ansel."

"Yeah, sure." Joe looked up. "Tohni, you aren't making much sense. Why would it matter who got them?"

"Because they're Reese's."

"Well, if you had them delivered to Ansel's office, why wouldn't Reese get them?"

"If Ansel's goons got their hands on those papers first, Reese could be in big . . . bigger trouble."

"Why?"

"Because he had documents that prove Ansel Chemical Corporation is guilty of midnight dumping. Reese knows where and when."

Joe squinted his brown eyes. "Midnight dumping? What's that?"

"Illegally dumping toxic waste."

"Illegal dumping, huh? Are you sure?" He pursed his lips and tapped his pencil on the desk.

"Yes. That's why Reese was running. And part of why Ansel wanted him. It had to do with this illegal dumping, not late alimony payments like we originally thought."

"How do you know so much about this guy?"

"Because Reese told me."

"Reese told you?" Joe repeated with slow

emphasis. Shaking his burly head, he scowled. "What is all this Reese stuff, Tohni? You two palsy-walsy? You sure got close to this case. Too damn close. I was afraid of that when you kept questioning me about Ansel Corporation. Then when you asked me about all those chemicals, I figured you knew too much." Joe wheeled around in his chair to file a manila folder in the cabinet behind his desk.

"Joe, I couldn't follow the man around for this length of time and not find out certain details about the case."

Joe whirled back around and fixed her with a steady stare. "Yes, you could. Your job is to stay cool and detached, Tohni. That's what you're paid for. You don't need to know why or how. Your only concern is who and where."

"Well, I did my job, didn't I? I brought him back!"

"Yes, you did your job well, Tohni, as usual. It's finished. Now forget about it. Sit down over there at that desk and fill out this report. I don't want to hear any more about Reese Kreuger or Ansel Chemical Corporation. I have a million other *more important* things on my mind today."

Tohni silently took the forms from Joe. With a long sigh—but no promises to forget Reese Kreuger—she sat at the desk and proceeded to fill out her report on the case. She stole a sullen glance at Joe, who had poured himself another cup of coffee and was leafing through the morning paper. Obviously he had forgotten about the case and expected her to do the same. He found nothing unusual about the way Reese had been handled when they met her car. Or at least he wouldn't admit he did.

She smiled grimly to herself. *That's* what was bothering her. She didn't want anyone pushing Reese around like that. If anyone put hands on him, she wanted it to be her. Oh, dear God, what a ridiculous thought! She would never get a chance to put her hands on him again. The last time had been to throw him roughly to the floor. *The last time* . . .

"Hey, Tohni, look at this!" Joe's voice boomed across the small office and she was jolted out of her reverie. " 'Playboy Found Intoxicated and Mugged.' "

"So?" She hadn't gotten very far in her paperwork and continued filling out her report form.

"It's your man, the one we've been discussing. Listen to this: 'A man identified as Reese Kreuger, former husband of heiress Gloria Ansel, was found intoxicated and unconscious yesterday.' "

"What? That's Reese! Oh, my God, Joe!" Tohni jerked out of her chair so fast she almost tripped. "They beat him up!"

"Take it easy, Tohni. The guy just got drunk and somebody mugged him. They found his empty wallet nearby. It's an obvious case."

"Let me see that!" Tohni tore the paper from Joe's hands and scanned the tiny article half hidden on the back page. "Oh, this is awful,

138

Joe. It was a setup! That's why they wanted us to bring him in! So they could do *this* to him!"

"You aren't making any sense, Tohni. Who is *they?*"

"Ansel's goons."

"Now why in the world would they do that? They just wanted to talk to the guy."

"I don't know exactly. But Reese considered them his enemies and this just proves it."

"Tohni, this is an open-and-shut case. The guy was drunk. Who knows what happened to him, and why? He was intoxicated!"

"No! He wasn't! He doesn't drink!"

"This article, which was based on the police report, says he was drunk." Joe tapped his finger on the desk for emphasis.

"Then the alcohol was forced into him, because I'm telling you this guy doesn't drink."

"Impossible, Tohni. Everybody in the jet set drinks."

"Not Reese. His mother is an alcoholic and he stopped drinking when he realized what she was doing to her life. This man doesn't drink more than an occasional beer or glass of wine. Joe, I've tailed him for weeks. I was his waitress every evening in Tennessee. When he needed to have a social drink he took tonic water with a twist of lime. No liquor."

Joe gave her a disgusted look. "Well, so? The guy doesn't drink. So he fell off the wagon this once."

"I don't believe that, Joe." Her gray eyes riveted defiantly on him.

"I believe you're too involved in this one, Tohni."

"Joe, don't you understand? I set him up for this. It's all my fault. Reese was almost killed because of me. And now he's in extreme danger."

Joe came around the desk and gripped her shoulders. "Tohni, snap out of it! This isn't your fault. You didn't set him up for anything. You couldn't know that he would get mugged after you brought him back to Atlanta. You're through with the case."

She shook her head. "Oh, no, Joe, I can't leave him like this. What if they come back and . . ."

He shook her slightly. "Oh, yes, you can leave him alone. And you will! You're finished with him. Come on, Tohni. Get a grip on yourself."

She took several deep breaths and stared at Joe. He must be right. He'd always been right. He'd been the best boss, the most interesting and knowledgeable man she'd ever known. From the minute she came to work for him five years ago, she'd respected him, admired him. My God, the man was a lawyer and the best damned investigator in the city. He was highly respected in the field. He had to be right.

So why did she feel like telling him to mind his own business and leave Reese Kreuger to her?

"Okay, Joe. You're probably right. Maybe he did fall off the wagon and get himself

140

mugged." Even as she said it, Tohni didn't believe it. At that moment she didn't know what to believe.

"Can we forget about this Kreuger and finish our work? I need that report you're playing around with. Why don't you finish filling it out, then take the rest of the day off. I have another assignment for you, but it can wait until tomorrow. It's easy. A simple job of bulldogging right here in town."

She nodded shortly. "Sure, Joe. You're right. I'll fill out this report and . . ." Her voice trailed off and she seated herself at the desk again.

Joe was right. She had to forget about Reese Kreuger and do her job. After all, she had other work to do. She'd always been proud of her ability to do her job well. Look how she'd trailed Reese, staying just clear of suspicion until the appropriate moment. She'd even managed to go to bed with him before he knew who she really was. Oh, what a devilish trick that was. And when he threatened to walk out, she'd proved to him she could handle the likes of Reese Kreuger, all five feet, eleven inches of him.

The delivery of her subject had been a cinch. There was a little trouble at the beginning, but with some gentle persuasion he'd come around to her way of thinking. Then she merely drove him down the highway, stopped the car, and let the goons take over. And they sure did. As surely as she was sitting here today, those damn goons beat him up. And left him for dead. And it was all her fault.

She sat bolt upright. They would only know he *wasn't* dead when they read the very article in the paper that she and Joe had read! And then they'd be back to finish the job! Oh, God, she had to prevent that!

Tohni scribbled furiously on the report form. In record time, she dropped it on Joe's desk. "Thanks for giving me the day off, Joe. See you tomorrow."

She sailed to the door.

"Tohni. You aren't going to do anything foolish like check on Kreuger in the hospital, are you?" His brown eyes stabbed accusingly at her.

She smiled innocently. "Why, Joe. Why in the world would I do a thing like that? I'm not responsible for every drunk that gets mugged. I think I'll go visit my mama. Haven't seen her in a long time."

Joe pursed his lips, then sent her away with a wave. "Tell Vera Lee I said hello."

"Okay. See ya." Tohni breezed out the door without a backward glance—nor an inner flinch for the lie.

If they hadn't known his identity at first, the ambulance would have taken Reese to the county hospital. He was probably still there, but a phone call would confirm it.

The hospital halls were hushed and smelled of alcohol and ether. In the distance she heard

142

a siren. It grew louder and louder until it stopped beneath the building.

She checked at the main desk for his name and room number, then rode the elevator to the sixth floor and hurried down the hall. Counting off the numbered doors, she halted before an end room. There was Reese's name on the medicine chart, bold and clear. She glanced around and removed the information sheet with his name, tucking it into her purse. It wouldn't do for anyone else to find him as easily as she had.

It had been two days since she had seen Reese, and the knowledge that he lay on the other side of this door made her heart pound. She could see his smiling, tanned face, so perfectly handsome, and those sky-blue eyes teasing her. But that was when she was Mandy Johnson. He hadn't been too happy with Tohni York. Would he be glad to see her? Probably not. They'd parted on not-so-friendly terms. She couldn't shake his parting look, the one he'd worn just before those goons shoved him into that limo.

Get a grip on yourself, she thought. You're cool, detached Tohni York, here to check on a subject. That's all. With a sweaty hand she pushed the door open and entered the room.

The sight of a battered Reese Kreuger, lying bandaged and helpless on the white hospital bed, sent her reeling to the wall. A wave of nausea swept through her and a lump the size of a fist choked her.

"Oh, my God, Reese honey! What have they done to you?"

CHAPTER NINE

One horrifying thought echoed through Tohni's head as she stared at Reese: *This is all my fault! He was nearly killed because of me!*

Slowly she moved toward him. When she finally reached the bed she was overwhelmed by a desire to wrap her arms around him, to hold him close, to give him comfort and relief from pain, to *keep him safe.* She who'd placed him in danger wanted to whisk him back to his hideaway on Lake Chickamauga. Oh, God, maybe she should have left him there. He was doing just fine before she entered his life.

Tohni touched his right arm, the one that wasn't in a cast. "Reese? Can you hear me? Oh, Reese honey . . ." Sudden tears sprang to her eyes.

His eyelids flickered, then lifted to reveal eyes filled with pain. No longer were they buoyant and blue like the sky. They were dull, and one was embedded in a purplish bruise. His nose—that perfectly straight nose—had been broken and was now covered by a white bandage.

He drew a quick breath as he recognized her. "Stay away from me, you little witch! I'm in no position to defend myself!"

Tohni blinked furiously and swallowed the impulse to vindicate herself. Another urge took over, a rush of love for this man. Gingerly, her hand grazed his taped ribcage and touched his bare shoulder. She wanted to touch him all over, but didn't dare for fear of hurting him more.

She hovered over him, then bent to kiss his cheeks, his forehead, finally ever so gently his lips. Tears rolled freely down her own smooth cheeks, and she wiped them away quickly so they wouldn't fall on him. "Reese honey, I'm so sorry. I had no idea they'd do this to you."

"Don't touch me!" he said tightly, and turned his face away from her. Even that small movement brought a grimace of pain to his face.

Her voice was a hoarse whisper. "Reese, please accept my apology. I feel so bad about all this."

"What are you doing here? Salving your conscience? Go away."

"I'm not salving anything." She looked down at her twisting hands and reconsidered. "Yes, maybe I am. But I . . . want to help."

"I can do without your kind of help, thanks. I might not survive it next time."

Her sad eyes moved over his bruised body. "No, I will help this time. When I saw the article in the paper I had to come here to see you."

"Well, now you've seen me. Satisfied? Good-bye!" He still refused to look at her.

"Reese, I can't leave you like this. I feel so responsible."

He chuckled with a raspy sound that ended in a raw cough and an ominous rumbling deep in his chest. "Spare me your confessions. If you're looking for absolution from me, forget it. Relieve your own guilt. You didn't do this. You just set me up for it. Now let me alone, Mandy. Or whoever you are."

"My name's Tohni." It wrenched her heart that he didn't bother to try to remember her real name. It only proved the extent of his disgust for her. She raised her chin and vowed stoutly, "I'd rather seek vengeance than absolution for my guilt. We've just got to figure out a way."

"Please, no more of your lying schemes."

Her hand slid down his arm and gripped his limp hand. "Reese, I know who beat you up. We'll get them. I swear."

"Well, you're the only one in town who does know. I tried to tell the cops and they laughed at me. It's hard to believe a crazed drunk with a broken nose and a black eye."

"You weren't drunk, were you?"

"Hell, no!"

"I didn't think so." She gazed at him with admiration. "Well, I'll corroborate your story to the police, Reese. I'll help you—"

"Forget it, Man—Tohni." He turned his face to her, and the hatred was clearly visible in his

147

dark eyes. "Can't you get it through your thick head that I don't want your help? I want you to leave me the hell alone. If there's anything I can't stand, it's a liar. You're about the best I've ever seen."

Tohni swallowed her pain at his harsh words. It was an acid compliment that stung deeply because it was true. "I can understand your bitterness toward me, Reese. I'd like to make it up to you."

"Bitterness is mild for the way I feel about you right now, Tohni. Make it up to me?" He paused to grimace as he shifted slightly on the bed. "How about tackling the entire Ansel Corporation? For all I know, they've sent you up here today to spy on me. Well, like what you see? You can report back that I'll keep my mouth shut for about as long as it takes me to get out of here and get my material organized."

"They didn't send me, Reese. No one did. This was my own idea. I had to know how you were."

"I'm in pain, that's how I am."

She squeezed his hand gently. "Then let's ask the nurse for something for your pain."

"I can do my own asking, thanks."

Tohni tightened her lips. He'd said something that triggered her mental instincts into overdrive. *Tackle the whole Ansel Corporation.* Well, maybe she would if she had to. If Reese stayed here in the hospital much longer, she might be forced to. Anyway, she had to do something quick, and she would.

"Right now, Reese Kreuger, you need me more than you care to admit. You're in a bind, to say the least. You need me whether you like it or not. And you've got to trust me because there is no one else for you to trust. I'm the only one who can help you." She paused to prop her fists on her slim hips. "And I assure you I was not sent here today by the Ansel Corporation. Nor was I sent here by my own investigation agency. In fact, if my boss knew I was here right now and what I was planning, I'd probably get the ax."

"Planning? Heaven help me from your scheming."

"First I'm going to get something for your pain."

"Just who do you think you are? My keeper? I don't want anything for pain! You are the source of my biggest pain. The one in my side! I don't want you around me. How much clearer can I say it?"

"You made it pretty clear," she acknowledged, with a pat on his arm. "However, I'm afraid you'll have to put up with me. Like it or not, I'm the only one around. And you're in no condition at present to help yourself. Not yet anyway. So I guess I am your keeper."

The word *keeper* rolled around and around in her head. Tohni knew she was the only one who could keep him safe. But how? By maintaining a constant vigil by his bedside? What if

Ansel's men tried to threaten him again? What if they came up here to the hospital? What could she possibly do to stop them? Reese was so damned vulnerable; with his bandages and painful bruises and broken bones, he couldn't even defend himself.

She had to do something to help him. But what?

Slowly a plan of action began to form in her mind. There were still some hitches in it, but those could be worked out. First she had to talk to the nurse and find out his exact status. Critical, serious, or stable? He looked pretty stable to her. Except, of course, for being in pain. What kinds of medication did he need? What kind of treatment would speed his recuperation?

Then she would need to know where various departments in the hospital were located, like the X-ray department, the lab, and the emergency room. She might have to make a quick side trip and needed to be prepared. And where did they keep extra wheelchairs?

She glanced at Reese again. No broken legs. That was good. He had been attacked on his upper body, which meant, perhaps, that he could walk. His lean form was covered, but from the ominous dark shadows visible in certain places, she figured he was nude underneath the thin white sheet. She'd have to rectify that. Maybe one of those flappy-tailed hospital gowns, open up the back, would do. Quickly she dismissed that thought. No, Reese

150

wouldn't stand for that. Better nude. And nude wouldn't work either.

"Can you walk, Reese?"

He opened his eyes and glared at her for a moment. "Walk? Why?"

"I'm serious, Reese. Is anything down there broken? Legs or feet?"

"No. As a matter of fact, I've strolled to the bathroom a couple of times."

"Good," Tohni muttered, nodding her head and drumming her fingers on his bedside table. Her mind churned. "Okay, what else?" She directed the question to herself.

"Nothing else! Go home!"

"I have too much to do here. You rest. I'll talk to your nurse about some medication. That should keep you quiet awhile."

It would also give her time to set her plan into motion. A gleam of determination lighted her gray eyes as Tohni darted out to the nurses' station.

Reese watched her leave with relief. Aside from hurting all over, he ached inside over what she had done to him. He had believed her. And it had been his undoing. His feelings for her were so confused, especially today. She was the same pixie-faced woman he'd found irresistible on the boat in Tennessee, the same one he'd lured to bed in the cabin. She was the same little beauty whose gray eyes haunted him at night and wouldn't leave his memory.

He made a fist with his one good hand. She was also the one who'd lied through her teeth to him. How could he have been so stupid as to believe her?

Never again! He'd learned his lesson the hard way!

A noise at the door drew his wide-eyed attention. Tohni had found a nurse and the two chatted merrily as they entered his room. He gave the women a quick double-take. Five-feet-two Tohni seemed even smaller beside the nurse who looked like a linebacker for the Pittsburgh Steelers! And she wouldn't even have to bother with shoulder pads to make the team! Her mitt of a hand was almost the size of a tray she carried with a vial of medicine and a sinister, gleaming syringe. Somewhere, he was sure, there was a needle lurking.

Damn them anyway. To hear these two women laughing and chatting, you'd think they were going to a party. What nerve! How could they be so happy when he was so absolutely miserable? He closed his eyes and moaned softly, praying they'd go away.

But of course they didn't.

"Mr. Kreuger, your cute little fiancée is concerned about you. She says you're in a lot of pain. I'm Beulah, and I have something here to relieve—"

Reese's eyes popped open. "My what? Fiancée? She's lying! She's not my—"

Beulah's hand rested on his shoulder like a twenty-pound weight. "I'm going to make you feel so much better, but first we'd better take a little trip to the bathroom. The medicine

152

might make you too dizzy to go later." She pushed a button and the head of the bed began to lift.

"That woman is not my fiancée!" Reese protested. "Just ignore her! And I do not need to go to the bathroom right now! I'll be the one to decide when I need to go, and then I'll do it myself." Reese felt out of control, sure that he wouldn't be deciding any such thing. Beulah would decide. And that little hellion with the sweet face standing beside her. Fake! They were all fakes! Oh, God, he was losing it! And it hurt like hell to sit up.

Beulah smiled patronizingly. "Please, sir. Do you need me to help you?"

"No, I don't need help," he snapped, and cast Tohni a disdainful look.

"All right, Mr. Kreuger. Go ahead yourself." Tohni hid a devilish grin behind her hand.

Reese saw nothing humorous about the situation. "Listen to me. That woman is not my fiancée. I don't know why she told you that, but it isn't so. And I don't need to go to the bathroom. Nor do I want a shot."

"Why, Reese honey," Tohni drawled breathlessly. "Don't you even remember me?" She turned a worried expression to the nurse. "Do you think this accident has affected his memory? Oh, my, honey!" She patted his knee affectionately.

"Don't you worry your little head now," Beulah soothed, talking to Tohni as if Reese weren't even there. "Patients act funny some-

153

times, especially when they're in pain. Like this one. He's probably just a little upset to find himself in the hospital all messed up like this."

Tohni's mouth formed a perfect O and she gave Reese's knee another pat. This time her hand was *under* the sheet!

"I'm not a little upset. I'm a *lot* upset to find myself beaten to a pulp! And to find you two females hovering around me like vultures!" Reese heaved a frustrated sigh.

"Reese baby, be a good boy and do what the nurse says," Tohni cooed, rubbing his knee.

"Take your hand off my knee! Look at her hand! She's a sex maniac!" He shook his leg like a bull trying to get rid of flies, but her hand stayed.

"This woman is crazy. She looks like an innocent little girl, but she's a real hellion! One of the best liars I know. And she packs a wallop with those little hands."

Tohni squeezed his knee sharply. "Reese honey, you're embarrassing me. I can't believe you're calling *me* a sex maniac when you—"

He looked wildly at Beulah. "Do you know that little squirt flipped me to the floor? She's really dangerous!"

"Reese honey, don't tell all our secrets," Tohni murmured sweetly. "Beulah, do you think he's hallucinating? He's never been like this before."

Beulah gave Tohni a quick nod and hid a smile. "Now don't you worry about a thing,

154

honey. We'll take care of him and get him back to bed. That shot will calm him down."

"I don't want a shot to calm me down! I don't want you females near me!"

"Easy now. Swing your legs off the side of the bed. Then just sit still for a minute until you get your bearings."

"Oh, hell!" Reese gritted his teeth as they propped him up. "Aaggg! My ribs! My head!"

"For someone so beat up he sure is mouthy. He isn't a very good patient, is he?" Tohni whispered loudly to Beulah. "It's because he's used to being in charge."

"That's what happens to these macho fellows," Beulah explained, obviously delighted to be the one in charge. "Come on, now, Mr. Kreuger. Let's go."

"Now wait just a damned minute!" Reese had had it. "I don't have any clothes on!"

Tohni looked at Beulah and shrugged. "I don't mind if you don't."

"Honey, I've seen everything in my day," Beulah said with a casual flip of her hand.

"Well, I mind!" Reese bellowed. "Get my pants!"

"Maybe we'd better get him something," Beulah conceded. "We don't want his blood pressure shooting up."

"If I ever get out of this, Mandy, I'm going to—"

"There he goes again. Can't even remember my name. What about a towel? Would that do

155

for now, Reese honey?" Tohni reached for a small hand towel.

"Tohni, then! For God's sake! At least give me a bath towel!"

"My, my, testy, aren't we?" She made a clicking sound and casually thrust the larger towel into his one good hand. Stepping back, Tohni watched carefully, taking mental notes on the process, as Beulah helped Reese inch across the floor.

By the time he returned to bed he'd decided to end the pain—and his awareness of the two women. Brazenly, he exposed a bare hip for the needle. "Sock it to me."

Tohni sighed with relief as Reese settled back down after the shot and appeared to go to sleep. "Thank you so much, Beulah. He was getting a little out of control. Now tell me the truth. Just what is his condition. . . ."

She strolled out of the room and down the hall with Beulah, gleaning every speck of information she needed. With a wicked smile on her darling, pixie face Tohni realized that Reese was right. She was a remarkably good liar. But sometimes it came in so damned handy.

Scarcely an hour later Tohni returned to room 613. She scooted past the nurses' station with her head turned the opposite way. Then she rolled her prized acquisition, an empty wheelchair, into Reese's room. In her hurry she knocked into the door, the wall, and finally the bed.

The clatter woke him up.

156

"What the hell? I thought I was rid of you for good."

"Hi! Feeling better?" She smiled generously. "I hope you're in a better mood now. You were as growly as a grizzly bear an hour ago."

He looked at her, looked again, then covered his eyes with his one good hand. "Is that a nurse's uniform you're wearing?"

She grinned and twirled for him. "Like it? Fits pretty good too, except at the waist. I had to pin it over here."

"Why?"

"It's too loose."

He raised his head, then let it fall, letting out a wail. "I don't care where it's loose. Why are you wearing that nurse's uniform? Don't tell me you're also a nurse."

"No, I just look like one. It'll attract less attention for what I have to do."

"Oh, God," he lamented. "What's that? Somehow I feel like I'm going to be a victim again, nude and wrapped in adhesive tape in advance!"

"Will you be quiet? I have to get you out of here."

"Oh, no, you don't. I'm not going anywhere with you!"

"You have no choice, Reese. It's too dangerous for you to stay here."

"It's more dangerous for me to go with you! If you'd just leave me alone, I'd be fine."

"No, you wouldn't. What if Ansel's men come back and try to finish their job? It would

157

be simple for them to slip into this hospital and up to your room. I did it. No one would stop them from doing whatever they wanted to you."

"Beulah would."

"Beulah might not be around. Anyway, I have a plan."

"You're going to sit beside the elevator door with a bazooka and blow them all to hell."

She gave him a withering look. "I'm going to take you to a safe place so you can recuperate. A place where they'll never find you. You'll be perfectly safe, Reese."

"Where? The armory?"

She winked. "Trust me."

"You've said that before. Why does the phrase send chills up my spine? Oh, I know. It trips from the sugary lips of the best little liar in Georgia. No, best in the whole South!"

"Reese, please."

"Tell me what in hell you're up to, Tohni."

"Ah, at least you remembered my name this time."

"Well, what do you expect? When you insist on hanging around where you aren't wanted to remind me."

"When you see what I brought you'll be glad I'm here."

"I doubt it," he grunted, but looked curiously at the wad of green material in her hands.

She let it roll out to its full length. "They're surgeon's greens. Doctors wear them when they do surgery or deliver babies. They'll be great for you. They're easy to slip on, and then you just tie them at the waist."

"Surgeon's clothes? Are they sterile?"

"I doubt it," she said, giving him a small twist of a smile. "But they're clean. Now put them on so we can be on our way."

"Sure, I'll just hop into them. I can't wait to go off on another junket with you. The last one was such fun!"

Tohni shook the pants impatiently. "Please cooperate, Reese." She pushed the up button on the side of the bed, and his head began to elevate slowly.

"Why do I have the feeling I have no choice in this?"

"Reese honey, don't you understand it's for your own protection that I'm doing this? I'm sure Ansel's people read that same article Joe and I did. They might be here any minute. We have to get you out of here fast."

"If I wasn't so damned groggy from that shot I'd . . ."

"Come on, now, swing your legs over the side."

With effort he did as he was told. Somehow fighting the little hellion didn't seem reasonable today.

"First the shirt. Then your pants. Come on now, Reese. Hurry."

She thrust the green items into his hands and waited for him to don the clothes. She tried not to pay attention to his sinewy calves with their curls of sandy hair, the muscular thighs, the

159

masculine prominence still hidden by the sheet. But the woman in her noticed.

"Now, stand up."

"I can't. I'm too dizzy."

"I'm right here beside you. Hold on to me. And the bedrail."

"In case you haven't noticed, I only have one good hand."

"Hold on to me when you stand up. Then turn around and sit in the wheelchair. This'll be quick."

"And it won't hurt a bit," he grated, moving to do her biding.

Struggling, swaying slightly, he lifted his hips off the bed. His one good arm clung to Tohni's shoulders.

She braced under his weight. Just touching him in such a caring way made her wish things were different between them.

"Tohni, get a move on. I'm dizzy."

Tohni pulled the wheelchair as close to him as she could and clamped the brake. "Just turn around and sit in the chair."

He did as instructed and she helped him get as comfortable as possible. As they breezed past the nurses' station, someone asked, "Is that six-thirteen?"

"To X-ray," Tohni answered without slowing her pace.

Reese closed his eyes. Otherwise he'd have to watch as his kamikaze driver wheeled him through the hushed hospital corridors like a bat

160

out of hell. "I hope you know where you're going."

"Trust me," she whispered in his ear.

He made a low, guttural sound.

Pushed around by a tiny, bustling, dark-haired "nurse," the once-proud, handsome man sat stoically with a white bandage on his nose. A single black eye. Bruises. One arm in a cast. Ribs thick with tape. Surgeon's green pants and shirt. Barefooted. Not too strange.

All things considered, the pair attracted little attention as Tohni brought him to the first floor. Abandoning the wheelchair in a maintenance closet, she pointed him toward the rear exit door frequently used by doctors and nurses. Surprisingly, no one noticed as she helped Reese outside and into her waiting car.

Tohni hurried around and slipped behind the wheel. By the time Reese was settled and had slammed the door shut, she had the car in gear and moving.

"Tohni, where are we going?"

"Just relax, Reese. I'll take care of you."

"That's what got me in this fix in the first place." He leaned his head back, not because he was relaxed but because he had no choice. The effects of that shot had left him dizzy. And so sleepy. Weak and vulnerable. Putty in the hands of this maniacal little female. "Come on, Tohni, tell me where?"

She glanced at the black-and-blue form slumped next to her. "Don't worry, Reese. Where I'm taking you, someone will take very good care of you. You'll be perfectly safe this time. I promise. Perfectly."

"Perfect . . ." he mumbled, drifting off in spite of himself.

Tohni drove like a madwoman, up and down streets, backtracking, circling. Everything else would be in vain if someone was following her, so she had to make sure. Her instincts worked overtime. She'd almost gotten him killed once. She couldn't let it happen again.

It took twice as long as it normally did, but finally she pulled into the driveway beside the elegant Georgian house. She rushed to the door, knocking furiously. "Mama! Stella! I need some help out here!"

CHAPTER TEN

It took considerable effort, but the three women managed to carry Reese to the large upstairs bedroom. He lowered himself to the bed with a moan, nuzzled the pillow, and drifted again into oblivion.

Vera Lee sighed. "It's sort of nice to have a man around the house, Tohni. Of course, this one is not exactly what I expected when you called."

Wait'll this one wakes up, Tohni thought. *You'll change your mind about "nice."* "They gave him a shot before we left the hospital, and I'm afraid it knocked him out. He was in quite a bit of pain."

Stella folded her substantial arms and walked around the bed, assessing Reese's physical condition. "Well, he sure is beat up bad, Miss Tohni. What in the world happened to him? Car wreck?"

"You hit it right the first time, Stella. He was beaten up," Tohni explained shortly. "Do you think you can take care of him? I'll help you of course. I talked to the nurse at the hospital and she thinks he'll be all right. It's just a matter of time for all of this to heal."

"Exactly what's wrong with him, Miss Tohni?"

Tohni tried to downplay the extent of his injuries by rattling them off fast. "Just a few cracked ribs, a fractured arm, shattered nose, bruises. He's going to be quite sore for the next few days. That's about it."

"My stars and garters!" Stella exclaimed, her dark eyes growing wide. "Why, this man's been beat to a pulp! It's a wonder there's anything left of him! I've never taken care of an injured man before. What can he eat? Can he do anything for himself?"

"Oh, he can take care of himself, when he's awake, that is. He can walk around and feed himself. He just needs a safe place to stay for a few days. That's all. These next couple of days will be the worst. After that, he'll probably recuperate fast. Don't worry about it, Stella. I'll be around. As far as food goes, fried chicken is his number-one favorite."

"You aren't just saying that because you'd like some of Stella's chicken, are you?" Vera Lee chided.

"Well, Mama, it does sound good." Tohni laughed. "Anyway, we want to keep our patient content and well-nourished, don't we?"

"Well, of course we have to think of the proper nutrition he'll need for the healing process," Vera Lee said seriously. "This man must have plenty of protein and vitamins."

164

"I wouldn't worry about it, Mama. He's strong and healthy. Whatever Stella fixes will be fine. All he needs right now is a bed to sleep in." *And a safe place to hide out in,* she added to herself.

Vera Lee approached the bed tentatively and peered over Reese as if she were inspecting an alien object that had dropped out of heaven. She turned innocent blue eyes to the other women. "He is a rather . . . healthy specimen, isn't he?"

Tohni hooted with laughter and winked at Stella. "Healthy specimen? Mama, please! If you mean that he has a good bod, I'll have to agree."

Vera Lee's blue eyes grew round. "Why, Tohni Lyn, I would never say a thing like that!"

"I know, Mama. That's why I said it for you."

Stella giggled as she swished her skirt and moved across the room. "I'm going right down to the kitchen and see what I can fix this man for dinner tonight. We don't want him losing any strength. You staying tonight, Miss Tohni?"

"Yes. And remember, Stella. Not a word about our star boarder. It's very important that we keep him a secret."

Stella placed her finger across her lips. "You don't have to worry about me, Miss Tohni. I won't breathe a word about him. Having a man around is a great secret!"

Vera Lee shook her head as Stella clomped down the stairs. "Tohni, I've never said very much about the young men you brought home, but this one's in pretty bad shape."

"Yes, he is, Mama. That's why I'm so grateful that you're willing to take him in."

"Did we have much choice, Tohni? By the time we saw what condition he was in, he was already here. Of course, we're always glad to help you out of a jam. You are in a jam, aren't you, sugar?"

Tohni nodded miserably. "Yes, ma'am."

"Is this the same young man you were stewing over the last time you were here?"

"I . . ." She paused and looked at her mother. Vera Lee was an amazing woman who seemed to be able to read her right down to the core. She sighed. "Yes, Mama. I've been worried about him for several days. You see, he was my subject, the one I was tailing up in Tennessee. I forced him to return to Atlanta. And he got all beat up because of me. So this . . . this problem is all my fault. I should have left him alone."

"Forced him?" Vera Lee gasped audibly and clapped her hand to her perfect rosebud mouth. "Oh, Tohni! You didn't do all this to him, did you? I never did like the idea of you learning that Japanese combat stuff! It isn't a very ladylike thing to do."

"No, Mama. I didn't actually do this. But I set him up for it. Delivered him to those who did it. That's why I have to hide him for a few days, just until things quiet down a little and he re-

166

gains some strength. Right now he's pretty helpless."

"And you feel guilty."

Tohni nodded miserably.

"But, sugar, you were only doing your job."

"That's exactly what Joe said. But, Mama, when I look at Reese and see all those bruises and broken bones, none of that matters. Look at what they did to him! It scares the hell out of me."

Vera Lee picked at the shoulder of Tohni's nurse's uniform. "Did you slip him out of the hospital? Is that why you're wearing this?"

Tohni nodded. "You're catching on to my little tricks, Mama."

"You always were one to take things into your own hands, Tohni Lyn. Right or wrong." Vera Lee looked back at the battered man. "Who is he, Tohni?"

"His name is Reese Kreuger. He's a toxicologist."

"What's that? Someone who stuffs animals?"

"No, Mama. You're thinking of a taxidermist. Reese deals with industrial chemicals in the environment. A few years ago he worked for Ansel Chemical Corporation. Unfortunately, he's threatened to report their illegal dumping. It could ruin their business."

"So they tried to shut him up."

"You've got it."

"They did a pretty fair job of it. Poor man." Vera Lee made a clicking sound with her tongue. "I'm not surprised though. Cornell Ansel has a reputation for being a real cutthroat in business. He'll do anything to make money."

Tohni looked mildly surprised. "How do you know about Ansel?"

Vera Lee shrugged. "He's been around for years. And, sugar, so have I. I've met him on several occasions. Charity balls and such. He's an arrogant, tight-lipped sort of man. I believe . . ." She paused and tapped her cheek with a well-manicured fingernail. "I think Reese Kreuger used to be married to Ansel's daughter."

"Nothing gets past you, Mama," Tohni admitted with a grim smile. "Yes. Several years ago he was married to Gloria Ansel. But they've been divorced almost two years. He and Ansel disagreed on business practices. Can you believe that he'd turn his ex–son-in-law over to goons? They almost killed him, Mama. I had to get him away from that hospital before they came back. To hide him until he can defend himself."

"Hide him? You mean you're hiding him here?"

"Where else could he go? Not back to his own apartment. They'd find him and—" She sighed and rubbed her hands helplessly on her thighs.

"Do you love him, sugar?"

There was a moment of pointed silence before Tohni answered. "I don't know, Mama. I . . . I just know I care very much about him. I ache inside seeing what they did to him. And knowing I'm responsible."

Vera Lee nodded. She had her answer, whether Tohni knew or not. And the words didn't tell her. The eyes did. She wrapped a motherly arm around her daughter's shoulders. "Looks like Mr. Kreuger will be out for a while. Let's see if we can find you some other clothes."

They left Reese sleeping peacefully.

"I'm telling you, Joe, we set him up. No, I set him up. I don't like it one bit."

"Tohni, we're in this together. You were just following orders. Anyway, we had no way of knowing what they wanted with him. We're hired. We do a job."

"I can't do a job that makes me an accomplice to murder."

"For God's sake, Tohni, it wasn't murder!"

"They intended it to be!"

"Tohni, I warned you not to get emotionally involved."

"Too late, Joe."

"Oh, hell. What does that mean?"

"Nothing. It's just that I can't help how I feel."

Joe ran a rough hand over his face. "And how's that, Tohni?"

She placed her hands on his desk and leaned toward him. "Like a heel. Joe, if you could only see him, you'd—" She broke off and moved away from his desk. Damn! She'd slipped! Usually she lied easily. That's one thing Reese hated so much about her. So why couldn't she just keep her mouth shut with Joe? All she had to do was keep quiet.

Joe stood and loomed over her, large and forbidding and damned angry. "You've seen him, I take it!"

"Let me explain, Joe. . . ."

"Yeah, you do that. I'm dying to hear why you broke my main rule and purposely disobeyed me yesterday. I told you *not* to go to that hospital! And you lied to me, damn it! You said you were going to see your mother!" His face was livid.

"I did. I saw Mama yesterday, Joe." She wouldn't tell him her mother was harboring an injured fugitive.

"But you also saw that Kreuger guy. Didja talk to him?"

"Yes." She didn't have to tell him their conversation was none too friendly.

Joe stuffed his hands in his pockets and took several deep, calming breaths. "How is he?"

"Broken nose. Beaten up face. Broken left arm and several cracked ribs. He's in bad shape, Joe."

"I guess the police are on it now. Are we going to be implicated by the investigation?"

"No, matter of fact, they wouldn't believe his accusations. When you think about it you can't really blame them. A guy who smells and acts drunk is beaten to a pulp and accuses a big company like Ansel Corporation of having him assaulted—it doesn't carry much weight. The story isn't very plausible."

"Drunk, huh?"

"He wasn't drunk. I told you that at the beginning."

"And you still believe it."

"I know it's true. Joe, Reese Kreuger is an honest man." Which was more than he could claim about her.

"I don't care if he's an honest man or a drunk."

She drew up taller and countered her boss. "You do care. Why'd you ask about him if you didn't care?"

Joe cast her an angry glance, his intense eyes cutting into her. "I only asked because I knew you'd been there. And I'm trying to understand how all this got so out of hand. Was it your fault or mine? Just how many times have I quoted my number-one rule, Tohni?"

"About a million in the five years I've known you."

"From the very beginning I've said, 'Don't get involved.' That first time you heard me speak at your law school I said it." He gestured emphatically as he stalked around the room.

"And practically every day since," Tohni groaned.

"So what do you do? The minute I turn my back, you prance over there and involve yourself with a guy who got himself beaten up. Damn it, Tohni, do you know what happens now?"

She shook her head.

He wagged his finger at her. "You're in danger, same as Kreuger is. You're in trouble with Ansel, along with your subject. I don't give a damn about Kreuger, but I do care about you! Now I've got to worry about one of my employees getting picked off because she's involved with some character who made a client mad."

"Don't worry about me, Joe. I can take care of myself."

"So could Kreuger, until they hired a bunch of thugs to work him over—*if* that's what actually happened. I don't want you going near him again, Tohni. The risk is too great."

"Joe—"

"Tohni, I'm serious. I don't want you hurt. Or worse."

She motioned in the air accusingly. "You just don't want to have to train another female operative."

"Training isn't my problem, little lady. I don't want to have to go to Vera Lee and explain anything tragic."

"Oh, Joe." She waved him off.

"Don't see him again, Tohni. That's an order."

"I won't go near the hospital again, Joe. That's a promise."

"Okay. Don't let anything like this happen again. Enough said about that." He rubbed his large hands together nervously. "Uh, how's Vera Lee?"

"Huh? How's Mama?" Tohni jerked her

head up and shrugged. Did he know that she'd left Reese at her mother's? "Why, she's okay."

"Well, you said you saw her yesterday."

"Oh. Yes. Yes, I did. Why, she's doing just fine, Joe."

"Tell her . . ." He paused and pulled on his ear. "Tell her I have some of that special fertilizer for her roses."

"Huh? What?"

Joe smiled self-consciously. "We were talking about flowers a few weeks ago and she wanted to know what I use to make my roses grow so big."

Her voice grew soft, and she smiled. "I didn't know you grew roses, Joe."

"Aw, I won a couple of ribbons in shows, that's all. Funny hobby for a big roughneck like me, huh?"

"No, I think growing roses is a fine hobby, Joe." Tohni scratched her chin thoughtfully. Was there more here than rose bushes and fertilizer? "And I'll tell Mama what you said. Next time I see her."

"You do that, Tohni." He tore a sheet of paper from the duty roster. "Here's your next assignment. This woman works at a bank. Her husband thinks she's seeing someone after work. Check it out."

"Okay." Tohni studied the paper, then looked up. "Joe? Thanks." Before he had time to answer she was off, wondering why he hadn't fired her. After all, she had broken the

173

number-one rule. And she intended to break it again.

Every evening Vera Lee met Tohni at the door with a brief update on Reese's condition. Then it was up to Tohni to try to get through his shell of hatred for her. It wasn't working too well. Oh, he was beginning to heal all right. But his cynicism was intact.

"How is he, Mama? Still the same?"

Vera Lee nodded briskly. "I'm glad you're here, Tohni. I'm just leaving. Have to meet the girls for dinner and bridge. Stella's off tonight, but she left a casserole in the oven. Reese is out by the pool. Smile for him. He needs some cheering."

"He's still a bear, huh?" Tohni kissed her mother's proffered cheek. "Thanks for the warning."

"Not a bear, sugar. Just . . . anxious. Sort of pacing the floor. I think it means he's getting better. See you later." She laughed and waved.

Tohni ambled through the beautifully appointed house, picking up an apple on the way. Reese was sitting in a lounge chair beside the pool. Reading. Wearing only a swimsuit. Oh, God, he was damned handsome, even with his injuries. All golden brown and so lean.

"Hi," she said, chomping on the apple. "Driving everyone crazy, are you? That's a sure sign you're getting well, you know. Ah, I see you got that funny bandage taken off your

174

nose. Now your face looks like it's all one piece instead of a mask split down the middle."

He gave her a hard stare. "I waited all day to hear your assessment of my face?" With annoying indifference he turned back to his book.

She took a seat in a wrought-iron chair near his lounger. "How're you feeling?"

"Okay."

"I know you don't care for my opinion, but your face is looking much better."

"You like black eyes, I take it. And lumpy noses."

She bit her lip. His remarks were biting and nothing she said or did seemed to mitigate his scorn. "Did Jason come over to check on your injuries?"

He raised his head from the book. "Vera Lee's old family friend, Dr. Jason Bentley? Yeah. He came over last night and gave me a once-over. Your mother is amazing. She has connections with everyone."

"That's my mother." Tohni nodded. "Well? What's Jason's verdict?"

"He thinks I'll live. The rest will take time."

Tohni scooted her patio chair closer. "Reese, you're doing fine. You're recuperating nicely. I know that staying here is boring, but it beats the hospital, doesn't it? I didn't see a swimming pool on your floor."

"Yeah, this is better. If I could swim, it would be great. But I can't get this damned cast wet. About all I can do right now is wade around."

"You're getting a nice tan." Her eyes swept

over his golden body and she tried not to pay attention to the muscles or the inviting curls of hair on his broad chest. There was no longer any tape on his ribs. In its place was a beige-pink Ace bandage bracing the injured ribs. Oh, how she'd like to wrap her arms around him again and . . .

"You don't have to baby-sit me tonight, you know."

"I hardly think of you as a baby. More like a bear. Would you believe I want to be here with you? Though the Lord alone knows why. So you can rail at me instead of Stella and Mama, I guess."

He threw the book down in disgust. "I guess I have been pretty . . ."

"*Unbearable* is the first word that comes to mind."

"Well, hell, Tohni, what do you expect? I'm wasting time, lying around here."

"It goes along with getting well. Not too many days ago you were laid up in the hospital with a bodyful of injuries. Healing takes time, Reese."

"And that's working against me, and for Ansel."

Tohni leaned forward and touched his hand. It was an involuntary act but a caring one. And when their hands met they both became instantly aware of the tension between them. "What's wrong, Reese? Are Mama and Stella hovering too much? Sometimes they tend to overdo the nurturing bit. But you must under-

176

stand, it's been a long time since they've had a man around. Especially one so handsome and virile."

His blue eyes flickered with something short of derision. "This is handsome?"

"Used to be. Will be again."

"Don't patronize me. That doesn't concern me anyway. And it isn't them. It's me. I'm bored out of my mind. I want to be busy. There's work I need to be doing. There are two reports I have to complete for companies in Tennessee. And another for the University of Tennessee at Chattanooga. I want to jog or work out somehow. I want to be on my own. I'm going to leave."

"But you can't leave yet," she said in alarm. "Give yourself a little more time, Reese. It's been less than a week since you were injured. You have a ways to go yet."

"That's what's wrong. I know I still won't be well tomorrow. But Ansel is moving ahead at his own pace."

"You don't have to stay here forever, you know. I only brought you here when you were in bad shape so that Stella could take care of you. And to hide you. I figured Ansel wouldn't know to look for you here."

"Stella has been wonderful. So has Vera Lee. It's just me. I don't belong here anymore." He took his hand out from under hers, an obvious attempt to put some distance between them.

Tohni ignored his rebuke and tried to create a lighter mood. "You'll miss Stella's cooking."

"Yes," he admitted. "She's great."

"Mama hasn't been too overbearing, has she?"

There was a tiny light in his eyes when he spoke of Tohni's mother. A light—at last—in those dull, sad eyes. "Vera Lee is a special lady. She's excellent company. Taught me to play bridge. Showed me her prize roses and gardenias. Do you realize she's quite a gardener?"

"I see she's captured you already. My mother has certain refined skills in dealing with men."

"Vera Lee? Why, she seems almost innocent."

"That's called southern charm, and she has always used it to her distinct advantage."

"Tohni, you make it sound as if she's actually devious. I find that hard to believe."

Tohni raised one eyebrow. "She's outlived three wealthy husbands. And has done very well for herself in life. Southern charm in action."

Reese smiled—actually *smiled*—for the first time in days. It seemed ironic that talk of Vera Lee would bring about that reaction. Or maybe it was typical. She did have a way with men. "Well, I'll be damned," he admitted slowly. "Could it be I'm intrigued by an older woman?"

Tohni smiled teasingly. "Why not? Mama *is* attractive. And wealthy."

"I've already had my fling with a wealthy

178

woman, remember?" he scoffed. "Somehow it's left a bad taste in my mouth."

She nodded solemnly. "Yes, I can see how it would. Still, my mother could probably give us both advice."

"Oh, really? Like what?"

"Well . . ." Tohni sighed and squeezed her hands together. "She would say if you had any sense you'd see that I care very much what happens to you or I wouldn't be risking my job right now."

"Spare me your hearts and flowers," he said with scorn. "This is your guilt trip, not mine!"

"At least I feel guilt!" she exploded, then turned away quickly. She continued in a lower tone. "But I realize I've made some mistakes too, Reese."

"Remarkable hindsight you have," he grumbled.

"I realize that right from the first I did and said all the wrong things with you."

"Oh?" He feigned surprise. "I would never have guessed it. All along I thought you were so sincere."

"I know you don't believe this, Reese, but I was sincere. Even though"—she paused to take a deep breath—"even though I lied to you. That's a real no-no when you're trying to build trust. And the next grand mistake was going to bed with you before either of us had made any commitments. Bad move. I know I've hurt you terribly. Any southern belle with the proper training would say that's enough to

179

ruin any relationship. If there was ever a relationship to ruin." Her gray eyes were dark and serious.

"Relationship? Ha!"

"Damn it, Reese, any decent southern gentleman would forgive a lady if the reasons were solid enough. And she apologized."

"Was that an apology?"

"Yes."

"Then I guess I'm not a decent southern gentleman. But then you"—he rose and approached her, touching an accusing finger to her chin—"you are no lady."

She swallowed hard; her eyes smarted at the accusation. "Don't you realize, Reese Kreuger, I would never have hurt you in a million years?"

He glared at her for long, agonizing minutes. Then he pulled her roughly against him with his one good arm. It was as if he couldn't resist touching her.

She leaned against him.

The kiss was rather clumsy and hard. His lips ground against hers, his teeth pressing into the tenderness of her lips. The ragged feelings of contempt and anger and bitterness came out in the meshing of their lips. And somehow those emotions turned into passion, a strong release of the feelings trapped inside him.

She pushed on his chest and forced them apart. "Reese, don't. You're hurting—" She stopped in midsentence, realizing that was exactly what he'd intended to do. Hurt her. And

180

she hated him for it. Hated, and yet understood.

And loved.

It was a strange realization as they stood so
close they could breathe the same air and feel
the pounding of each other's heart.

"Reese—"

She trembled against him, unable to pull
away. He lowered his head and kissed her
again, kissed her deeply, emotionally, their
damp bodies straining together. Her palms slid
up the hair-roughened contours of his chest to
his shoulders. Her searching fingers entwined
with the hairs at the back of his neck and she
molded her small, soft body to his.

His arms encased her, pressing her to him,
relishing her purely feminine response to him.
He wanted to bury himself in her, to crush her
to the floor, to make her feel the pain he'd gone
through. No, that was ridiculous! He simply despised her. Abruptly, and as roughly as he'd
embraced her, he pushed her away, muttering
a curse.

After a moment she moved toward him
slowly. Placing her hands gingerly on his
cheeks, she stroked softly. "I can understand
how you feel. All you have to do to hate me is
look at yourself in the mirror and see all these
bruises."

"I want to hate you," he admitted hoarsely.
"I can't help how I feel."

"I know." Something came over her as she
examined his face closely and looked into his

dark eyes. In the days since the incident he had begun to heal. The bruises had changed colors —but they were still there. Lumps and bruises. Broken bones. And he would never be the same again. There were some things that would never heal. Because of her. Emotion flooded her being and sudden tears filled her gray eyes. "Reese, I'm sorry," she whispered. "So sorry."

"Tohni, don't." He twisted from her gentle grip. "Don't push me any further."

Her voice then achieved a new calm. "I won't push you, Reese. I want to help you."

"Haven't you done enough?"

"Maybe not. I think I can help you. And keep you safe until you're ready to submit your reports to the EPA."

He looked at her anew. She wasn't asking forgiveness or wallowing in self-pity anymore. She was talking about action, it seemed, not about how to sit around passively waiting for bruises to heal.

"Exactly what are you talking about, Tohni?"

"I'm talking about working up a strategy for proving your charges against Ansel. And doing it quietly, until you're ready to release it."

"How?"

CHAPTER ELEVEN

Tohni turned away from him. He was still so indignant. He was a formidable opponent too, and as they talked in the deepening twilight he opposed her and every idea she presented. Well, she could be a fighter too. She inhaled deeply, trying to collect her thoughts and discard her twisted emotions. Could she do it? There was no question in her mind. *She had to*. It was her only way of holding on to Reese Kreuger, even for only a brief time and by flimsy ties.

"If you don't stay here, where will you go? What will you do?"

He shrugged. "I can always go to friends. There're plenty who'd be willing to take me in."

Tohni groaned inside. Of course there were. A man like Reese Kreuger had a world of friends who'd do anything for him. Many of them probably female too.

"But can they help you with your work?" she countered with a coolness she didn't feel. She still had another round to go in this fight and

183

anything could happen. "And can you trust them to keep quiet about you? And your work? If word got around about your whereabouts, it could be very dangerous for them. Don't you think Ansel's men are staking out your friends' places as diligently as they're watching your old apartment? I would."

His head jerked up. "Did you?"

"Of course." She gave him a sly grin and continued her verbal jabs. "How do you think I traced you so quickly to Tennessee? It wasn't too hard. Somebody thought I was an old girl friend trying to look you up."

"Who?" he bellowed, and pounded a clenched fist on the table. She was claiming that one of his friends had betrayed him! Could he believe her this time? "Who the hell told you where I was staying? I'd like to work him—"

"Un-uh," she cautioned, wagging a finger. "That's privileged information. I don't dare reveal my source. Anyway, what good would it do to tell you? Just break up a friendship."

"What good? A little revenge is good for the soul! If I could just get my hands on him!"

She smiled patronizingly and delivered her uppercut. "Oh, now, Reese. Is that any way to talk about friends? Anyway, it wasn't a he."

"A woman? Oh, hell!" Anger darkened his face and he stood to pace off his frustration.

Tohni lowered her tone as she moved in with her follow-up punches. "But don't you see, Reese? Your friend didn't realize she was get-

184

ting you in trouble. She didn't know what you were trying to do or why. She didn't understand the impact of your information and accusations. And she couldn't possibly know the consequences for the Ansel Corporation, therefore couldn't be expected to know the potential danger it posed. Or anything about Ansel's vicious tactics."

"Or yours."

His counterpunch hit her hard and she took a moment to recover. "Yes, but I know all those things. You need more time to recoup, Reese. Plus you need to be in a safe place. Your friends don't understand that."

"I realize I'm not up to full working potential by any means," he said slowly. "But I'm able to work and I can't do it here. I'll just get another apartment."

"You can't do that," she said, rebounding quickly. "You . . . you need too much help. What kind of work are you talking about?"

"Mostly typing and organizing. With this bum arm those jobs are practically impossible for me. I need to gather my information and document it properly before I can make an official statement about the Ansel Corporation. Now, of course, it'll include assault. I want to be prepared to take it to the EPA, the state legislature, the federal courts, newspapers, anyone who'll listen."

"Why don't you *sue* Ansel for assault? We could come up with proof."

"No. This issue is more important and far-reaching than a personal lawsuit. I don't want to waste my time with that."

"You wouldn't consider letting it all drop, Reese?" She looked at him hopefully.

His lips tightened and he spat the words out. "Not for a second."

"Reese, I'm afraid you're heading for more trouble."

"That's the nature of this game, Tohni."

"What you need is a . . . a bodyguard. Someone to keep you safe until you've finished your job."

"Bodyguard?" he repeated derisively. "Are you volunteering?" He gave her a scathing once-over.

"We-e-e-ll, I'd consider it." She pretended to mull over the idea.

"Great bodyguard you'd make." He laughed. "Look what happened to me last time." He gestured futilely at the Ace bandage around his ribs. He was broken and hurt because of her and wouldn't let her forget it soon.

"Yes, but they caught us unawares. Next time we'll be ready for them. I, uh, have a black belt in karate."

"I hope there isn't a next time, Tohni. I might not survive it."

"Then stop now, Reese, before it goes any further." There was a degree of pleading in her voice, but she didn't care. They were talking about Reese's life and she couldn't think of anything with a higher priority.

"I won't give up, Tohni." He looked at her with stout determination.

"You're a very stubborn man, Reese Kreuger."

"Only when I'm right. And this time I am."

She met his gaze with a stubborn look of her own. Then she smiled encouragingly. "I happen to agree with you, Reese. And I'd like to help."

"You want to get involved in this mess?"

"I already am." She moved closer and raised her head so he could see the seriousness in her gray eyes. "Move in with me, Reese. I could hide you for a little while. Nothing permanent, you understand. No commitments necessary. But you need time. To get well. And to decide what to do and how to get it done."

"Tohni, I know what I'm going to do. I just need help finishing the reports. Typing, organizing papers, et cetera."

"I could do that."

He raised his eyebrows. "Do you type?"

After a moment's hesitation she asked lightly, "Doesn't everybody?"

"With this broken arm, typing is one of my biggest stumbling blocks right now. Under normal circumstances I'd just hire a temporary secretary. But with these inflammatory and technical documents I'm not sure whom I can trust."

"The answer is simple, Reese. No one. I'm all you have left. You have to trust me."

"After our experience in Tennessee, that's a

laugh! I wouldn't even swear to your real name."

"Now, Reese, you know I was only acting in the line of duty."

"I only know you're a damn good little actress. And a pretty good liar!"

With his attitude their working arrangement wouldn't be easy. But she had to try. "If you moved into my apartment you'd have lots of privacy every day while I'm out to work. I have an extra room I use for sewing and storage. We could convert it into an office for you."

He hesitated, and Tohni knew he was giving the strange proposal consideration. Before he could refuse she went on quickly.

"Plus my apartment complex has a spa and gym. You could jog on a machine or exercise and use the spa for your rehabilitation. It's all enclosed, therefore relatively safe. No one would know who you were. Or care."

"You make it sound too good to pass up, Tohni."

"Then you'll do it? Great!"

"Whoa! Slow down! Did I say yes?"

"Any reasonable, clear-thinking person would know I'm right. You can't go back to your old apartment. You can't trust your old friends. Things are different now, Reese. Ansel's out to get you and he fights dirty. You have to fight smart or give up."

"You know I'm not giving up, Tohni." He ran his hand wearily along the back of his neck. "I suppose any red-blooded, clear-thinking male would jump at the chance to move in with you, Tohni. Only trouble is, I know you all too well."

"I'll make it up to you, Reese."

"I don't think you can, Tohni. But I guess I could do worse than to move in with a private eye who knows karate."

She smiled in triumph. "A good operative is ready for any situation that might come up."

Reese turned his eyes skyward and groaned, "Of all the private eyes in this city, why do I have to get stuck with this one?"

"You're just lucky, I guess," she replied with a big grin.

They moved him in that night, under cover of darkness. Tohni told Vera Lee that Reese was moving back home. She didn't say which home. And of course Vera Lee was too polite to ask.

"You're funny," Reese commented as they drove to Tohni's apartment. "For such an aggressive, self-appointed bodyguard, you sidestep your mother like she's the prima donna."

"Now, how could I tell my mama I was moving you into my apartment when I know it's against her principles?"

"Coward."

"I know," Tohni conceded with a wry grin. "But what can I say? She's my mother."

"Are you claiming you've never lived with a man before?"

Tohni pulled into a parking space below her apartment. "You're the first."

189

"If you'll pardon me for saying so, I wasn't your first man."

"Do you want a complete report? Actually, someone like you would find my love life dull. I had a lover once, but we never lived together. Nor did we do any globetrotting, like some people I've heard of."

"Touché."

"But our situation now is different, Reese. This is in the line of duty. A necessary situation. We have a job to do. That's it. There'll be separate beds and separate rooms," she stated firmly, and opened the car door.

He followed her up the stairs. "You make it sound like it's your patriotic duty to take me in."

"The way I see it, Reese, you have a special message to deliver to the people of this country, and I'm going to help you deliver it."

"And all this time I thought you were salving your conscience."

She received his accusation quietly and unlocked a door that led directly to her upstairs apartment. "Let's just say it's my way of apologizing for the trouble I've caused you."

He halted in the doorway. "Are you on a guilt trip again?"

"No, I'm over that. I just happen to believe that what you're trying to do is right." She smiled sweetly. "I promise I'll do everything in my power to help you, Reese. Including learning to type. Bring your suitcase in." She sailed breezily through the doorway.

He stared after her for a moment, then followed. Tohni's living room was the latest in clean, straight lines without a picture or mirror to clutter the stark, white walls. The furniture consisted of two bean-bag chairs and a sofa turned to a small TV.

The dining room wasn't much different. A table and four chairs. Surely they'd been used sometime, yet everything looked so pristine. Not an antique clock or silver tea service in sight. Nothing in Tohni's place was faintly reminiscent of her mother's elegantly appointed home with its gilded mirrors and crystal chandeliers. The kitchen looked unused.

"Tohni? Are you admitting you can't type? You said you could help me type those damned reports!"

"Don't worry. I'll help you type them. I use the two-finger hunt-and-peck system with amazing speed and accuracy." She paused in the hallway between two doors. "I said, 'Can't everybody type?' I just forgot to add, 'Everybody but me.' You won't really hold it against me because I can't type, will you, Reese?"

He looked at her grimly for a moment. "No. Anybody who has moves like the Karate Kid can't be all bad."

"I thought you'd be sensible about it. Your suitcase in there." She jerked a thumb toward one of the rooms.

"What in the world?" Reese dropped his suitcase near the door and gaped at the room.

"Your future office. I told you I used this room for sewing and storage."

"Somehow I imagined stacks of boxes and an old treadle Singer. Not the costume department for Universal Studios!"

Amazed, he walked into the room. Obviously this was where Tohni spent most of her time when she was at home. There was a stereo and a table laden with two Diet Coke cans and a half-empty bowl of popcorn. Everything seemed to center around the closet, which was permanently open as the doors had been removed. Extending from the closet and all the way across the room were two racks full of costumes. A very modern sewing machine perched on a long table which dripped odd pieces of material and patterns. The walls were covered with posters of people in native attire from all over the world. Her interest in and skill in making all kinds of costumes of the whole world were apparent. And extensive.

"Did you do all this?"

"I didn't make all of them. Some of them come to me by, uh, osmosis, like the nurse's uniform. And I just keep them in case I need them again. You never know in this business."

Reese lifted a sequined bra with several filmy scarves attached. He cast a questioning glance at Tohni.

"Belly dancer. Thank God I didn't have to do much dancing. I just popped out of a cake at a bachelor party where I was hired to keep an eye on the guest of honor and make sure he

192

remained faithful to his beloved. That was a dangerous night. Craziest bunch of men I've ever seen!"

Reese shook his head slowly and ambled on down the line of clothes. Pausing, he pulled out something familiar. White overalls and a purple sweater.

"Oh!" She smiled. "That's my collecting-for-cable-TV outfit. You remember that one."

He rolled his eyes. "I should have known there was something fishy about that collector. White overalls indeed."

"Aw, we understand about you scientist types. You're such deep thinkers, you don't see the obvious. At least that's what I was banking on." She grinned generously. "Worked too."

"Indeed it did. Where's the Dolly Parton wig? And the other part?"

Opening a drawer full of colorful scarves and belts, Tohni lifted out a bra fully equipped with an ample bosom. "I just put this on and *voila!* Instant curves! Wigs and hats in there." She nodded toward the closet.

From floor to ceiling shelves extended across the closet, with model heads wearing wigs or large, floppy hats. Coiffures in every shape, size, and color lined the shelves.

"Well, I'll be damned. I can't believe it." Reese walked slowly toward the closet. "You could be a different person every day of the week."

"Sometimes I am. My job often requires me to work incognito. I happen to enjoy being creative about it. I mean, you can only wear a cloche over one eye so often. Then it gets really boring. And the job can be boring enough as it is. So I make it as interesting as possible."

"With the likes of this?" He pulled out a complete gorilla costume. "Don't tell me. You were an extra when they filmed *Greystoke.*"

"Close." She grinned. "That costume's really been around. Every time I wear it, something interesting happens. It's good to wear because it allows you to be *completely* incognito. But it's hot as blazes because of all the fur.

"Once I wore it to a Halloween party where I'd been sent to observe some errant husband's extracurricular activities. Of course I wasn't invited, so I had to keep it on all night long. I nearly died from the heat. Someone flicked a cigarette my way and it caught fire! See this little hole?" She poked a finger into the leg and wiggled it. "While we were putting out the fire, my subject made hay on the back balcony with somebody's wife. He nearly got killed when her husband found out!"

"Dangerous job you have, little lady. Makes my contributions to your lively life seem almost tame."

"Almost." She nodded.

He turned around and looked at her strangely. "Who are you, Tohni York? When you step into this costume room you can be anybody you want, from a harem dancer to a gorilla. Which one is the real you?"

She shrugged self-consciously. "I'm none of

these. I'm just me. An ordinary little southern gal."

"Ordinary?" He propped his fists on his hips and glanced around the room. "There isn't an ordinary bone in your body, Tohni York. You're the most . . . surprising woman I've ever met."

"Is that a compliment?"

He looked at her and laughed contemptuously. "Compliment? The best compliment I could give you is that you hit like a sledgehammer."

She took a deep breath and turned away. What ever made her think he'd forgive and forget? Or that this little experience would be easy?

Later, around one, she made a trek to his old apartment to pick up his typewriter and papers. She slipped back with an official report. "Just as we suspected, your place has been ransacked. You're lucky they didn't touch these papers, Reese."

He flipped through the assortment she'd brought. "These are just on some random research. The important stuff on Ansel Corporation is locked up."

"Oh? Where?"

"My safety deposit box at the bank," he said.

"Very clever." She nodded with admiration for his foresightedness. "Well, what about all that stuff in your briefcase? I thought that was the information on Ansel."

"That's just the work I was doing in Tennessee. I told you I'm a consultant. That's what keeps the wolves away from the door. Several companies hired me to evaluate their toxic-waste disposal methods and I was in the process of compiling the reports when I was so rudely interrupted." He cast her an accusing glance. "Those reports are now due and I need to complete them. You say you have them, Tohni?"

"I hid the briefcase in my closet, thinking I had some explosive stuff on my hands." Proudly, she produced the brown briefcase.

"Fine." He smiled and opened the briefcase. His blue eyes gazed with satisfaction at the array of papers. Then he lifted his eyes to hers. Both of them remembered the disastrous morning when she'd broken the news that she was taking him back to Atlanta. They had thrown papers and clothes together helter-skelter and left Chickamauga in the rain. And Reese had ended up in an alley that night.

"Thanks, Tohni," he murmured. "I needed these."

"Sure, Reese." She lowered her eyes. It did no good to relive the miserable past. That was over and done with. So was their relationship. "Well, it's late. You, uh, can sleep on the sofa tonight. I'll see if I can borrow a roll-out bed tomorrow."

"Okay." He nodded curtly and snapped the briefcase shut.

During the next few weeks tension built like an impending storm. Tohni continued to work for Eagle Eye Investigations by day. Reese worked too, in the office half of the sewing room. Tohni found a roll-out bed for him and it now occupied a corner.

There were two positive results. Reese got his work done and his injuries healed rapidly.

However, time did nothing to stabilize the relationship between Reese and Tohni. If anything, their being together so much, with no warmth between them, made things worse. Reese was often snappish and irritable. Tohni was anxious. She knew their time together was limited. His leaving was something she dreaded, but knew was inevitable.

Every day she watched him grow stronger, and every day her fear that he would leave grew stronger. She knew it would come someday. And that day was looming closer and closer. She determined to cling to whatever they had together until then.

When the cast was finally removed from his arm, Reese was horrified by the shriveled muscles. He began a rigorous regimen in the gym to rebuild the muscles and to keep the rest of his body toned.

At night they compiled and typed his data on Ansel Corporation. It was a complicated process, and Reese was a taskmaster and difficult to please. Yet Tohni tackled her job with verve. It was something that had to be done. And she was committed to it.

197

One sweltering June afternoon Tohni arrived home from work early to find the apartment empty. Reese's desk was still littered
with papers. Obviously he intended to return
to his work soon.

So he was probably downstairs in the gym.
Sometimes he took a break like that. Tohni
kicked off her shoes and stripped off her
clothes, discarding them on the bed. She
tugged her jogging shorts on over her slender
hips, thinking how anxious she was to see him.
And how silly it was since they'd seen each
other just that morning over coffee. Of course,
neither had said very much. Still, in a strange
way, she looked forward to seeing him every
day. It hit her then how much she'd miss him
when he was gone.

She knew Reese was growing impatient with
his inactivity. His world was limited to her
apartment, the gym and spa downstairs, and
the deli across the street. She wondered if
there was any way they could forge their
worlds when this was all over. What would
happen to them then?

It was strange, but she wanted to be near
Reese, even though there was little to their
relationship. He gave her nothing, yet she was
emotionally tied to him. Was this love? The
sweet/hard, gentle/strong feelings she had for
Reese Kreuger were myriad, but did they add
up to love?

She slammed the door and took the stairs
two at a time. The gym was full with the after-

work crowd. Yuppies, southern set. She looked around, but no Reese.

Well, maybe the spa. She didn't spot him sitting in the steaming waters and stood impatiently by the door, thinking he might be in the bathroom. Or dressing room. Fifteen minutes later she gave up.

Her heart pounded heavily even as she began to jog across the street to the deli. When she didn't find him there she felt a flutter of panic in the pit of her stomach. She returned to the apartment, trying to keep calm. Should she call the police? No, there was nothing to report. Reese was a grown man. It wasn't even dark yet. She couldn't very well report him missing for thirty minutes. She tried not to panic.

But inside she was terror-stricken.

She slumped into one of the bean-bag chairs and flipped on the TV. As the nightly news began, she found herself hyperventilating.

She buried her face in her hands, trying to blot out the mental image she had of Reese lying in some dark alley, beaten and bleeding. *Oh, no! Reese! I love you! Don't get yourself hurt again!* Or worse.

A noise at the door drew her attention and she sprang to her feet. "Reese? Reese?"

CHAPTER TWELVE

"Damn it, Reese! Where have you been?"

A wave of emotion flooded through Tohni, threatening her usual cool reserve. He stood before her in gray jogging shorts and a yellow Georgia Tech T-shirt with a ridiculous black bee across the chest—and *he was perfectly fine*. No bloody nose or black eye. No bruises. No broken ribs or arms. He wasn't even out of breath, certainly not from rushing back to reassure her. He was infuriatingly casual.

Tohni was torn between the urge to grip his shoulders and shake him for causing her so much worry, and the desire to wrap her arms around him in a loving hug, grateful because he was all right. She wanted to scream and cry and laugh, all at the same time. But she did nothing, just kept it all bottled up inside.

"Out." He shrugged and walked by her.

She stared at his broad shoulders and was seized by the urge to grab and jerk him around. "Out where? Why didn't you tell me where you were going? Leave a note or something? You're late!"

He paused and turned around slowly to face her. Electrifying blue eyes flashed with rebellion in response to her sudden, uncharacteristic possessiveness. "Since when do I have to report to you whenever I walk out of your sight?"

She took a trembling breath, then quickly looked away. Her hands raked through her black curls, leaving them tousled wildly around her pixie face. "I—you're right, Reese. This is ridiculous. I don't know what got into me. I was just so . . . worried about . . . you." Her voice faltered at the end.

"Tohni? Are you all right?"

She pressed her lips together tightly and shook her head. Wrapping her arms around herself fiercely, she turned away from him. It was embarrassing, this rash and unmanageable display of emotion. In only a few second's time she had experienced both nerve-wracking fear and unreasonable anger. She had railed at him like a jealous wife, demanding to know where he'd been. And now she was possessed with a crazy urge to melt inside and cry like a baby.

In that moment the blue eyes softened. Electrical tension, building for weeks and threatening to ignite within them both, became a thread that drew them together.

He reached out for her, his large hands resting heavily on her quivering shoulders. "Tohni . . . Tohni . . ."

She turned quickly into the circle of his comforting arms and eagerly wrapped her arms about him and pressed her ear to his heart.

He felt warm and wonderful, and she was finally where she wanted to be. Gratefully, she inhaled the special masculine essence that was always a part of Reese. It followed him as he stalked through a room and centered on him as he worked at his desk. The fragrance gave her a heady solace and she relished the intoxication. The slow, rhythmic pounding of his heart against her body was solid and reassuring.

He was all right. Safe!

"You're absolutely right, Reese," she finally managed to mumble against the broad spread of his chest. "Of course you don't have to check in with me every minute. I shouldn't have grilled you like that. I don't know what happened to me. But when you weren't in your usual places, something snapped in me and I . . . I sort of panicked."

"You?" He chuckled gently and she felt it vibrate through her body. "My calm, cool private investigator who's clearheaded in any situation—panicked?"

"My imagination went crazy. I was afraid they'd hurt you again." She squeezed her eyes shut to force away the terrible image that still haunted her.

"Hey, Tohni, you can't do this every time I'm out of your sight. You'll drive yourself crazy."

"I know." She sniffled and pressed a wet kiss through his shirt to the cushiony mat on his chest. When she realized what she'd done, she

202

froze. How could she do such a thing? Show such affection for this man who despised her so?

But Reese pretended it was entirely natural. "What's this? Tears?" He lifted her chin and lowered his face to hers. Within inches he stopped. "Tears for me?" he whispered dubiously.

She forced a faint smile. "It sure messes up a bodyguard's ego for her subject to disappear."

"Bodyguard?" His thumb stopped a tear that had trailed all the way down her cheek to her neck. He caressed the moist area, inadvertently spreading the trail. But the motion did nothing to check the flow.

Without finishing his thought of her as his bodyguard or her railing at him and crying, he closed the space between their faces and kissed away the tears. His lips brushed her nose and the moist areas of her jaw and cheeks, moving over her skin in hypnotic fashion. He couldn't stop kissing her now that he had her, couldn't force himself away. Not just yet.

She stood immobile, unable to break away, her face turned up to his, gratefully accepting his lavish affection. Any bit of tenderness from him was so rare that she'd thought him no longer capable of it. But the sweetness revealed now in his heartfelt act was tinged with an underlying passion, and Tohni found it exciting.

She wasn't even surprised when his lips finally met hers. A salty flavor lingered on their

203

lips as he traced the shape of her mouth with his tongue. Warm and firm, he pushed it through to the far reaches of her mouth. And she accepted him eagerly.

They clung hungrily to each other. Tasting and touching and licking greedily as if it were an act of nourishment. Reese crushed her small body to his, seeking to merge them, to bury himself in her softness, to mold the contours of her femininity to his rougher, angular shape.

In some dark recess of her mind Tohni was aware of the excited part of his body as they stood enfolded like that, and she desired him with a yearning she'd never felt before. If he left her now, at this moment, she thought she'd surely wither away and die.

Then his lips were on hers no longer, but were forging a heated path down the sensitive column of her neck. He stopped at the neckline of her T-shirt.

"Tohni, what have we been doing to ourselves?"

"Oh, God, Reese," she said, breathing heavily. "I don't know."

"It's been hell without you."

He kissed her again, long and deep, and his hand slid under her shirt to cup one fine-pointed breast. Her silky skin, separated from his only by thin scraps of material, drove him to the point of distraction.

Their self-imposed celibacy had sent him to the gym to work out at many an odd hour. Sometimes the soft rustle of Tohni moving about her bedroom required him to take a cold shower at midnight. It was a life alien to him, something he'd never done, this holding back. He'd never lived with a woman he couldn't have. And he'd never lived with a woman he wanted more than this one. Now she was here against him, soft and willing. And yet he held back.

All along he'd told himself he hated her. That he couldn't possibly desire a woman who'd deceived him and set him up like this one had. And he knew she thought of him merely as a subject.

Oh, yes, she'd felt guilt when she set him up for the beating. And that's why she had taken him in. Guilt. Nothing more. And yet, at this moment, he was feeling more, much more. He was straining against her, aroused and hot, desiring her with a voracious hunger. A hunger that had been growing during weeks of famine.

"Tohni—" His voice was a soft rasp.

"Yes." There was a certain willingness in her tone.

His hand pressed the softness of her breast. "I want to touch you, Tohni." It was a statement, an obvious fact, but they were not beyond halting everything. He was giving her the chance to refuse. But he must have been crazy to think she didn't want him too.

She moved, not away, but in a writhing motion against the hot strength of his hand. Then she shifted and deftly peeled off her T-shirt and let her bra drop to the floor. Standing bare-breasted and shimmery in the growing shadows, she softly enticed him. "Touch me, Reese."

He needed no more encouragement. Simultaneously, his hands caressed both her breasts until the gentle swells burgeoned and the enflamed tips became distended and hard. Suddenly, touching her with his hands wasn't enough, devouring her with his eyes didn't satisfy, so he bent to kiss her creamy breasts and taste her strawberry nipples.

Tohni arched against his mouth and issued a soft, kittenish sound. The fires that had sizzled within her when she worked beside him, feeling his warmth, or when she handed him a cup of coffee and brushed hands, now surged into flames. Sometimes when he appeared in the mornings, his hair disheveled and eyelids sleep-heavy, she had to struggle to control the tiny flickers in her heart. But now, with him openly caressing her, all that energy and emotion were kindled to a raging wildfire that licked through her veins and left her weak.

She reached for him and held on to his waist for support as his tongue caressed her breasts and his hands skillfully slid her jogging shorts and panties down past her thighs. Unnoticed, they dropped to the floor and his hands continued their maddening caress of her thighs and hips and waist. When one hand moved across the flat of her tummy, she thrust forward to meet the pressure of it against her mound of pleasure.

"Oh, Reese—" she moaned.

For a brief moment he stopped touching her. She opened her eyes to see that he was only removing his shirt. She pressed her lips to his chest, burying kisses in the mat of hair, along the swell of his muscles, on each button-hard nipple.

Then slowly she sank to her knees, her hands scraping over his buttocks and taking his shorts down. Shamelessly she planted kisses along the way, and when she reached her knees he was kneeling with her, his thighs tightly embracing hers.

His face was dark with passion and he looked directly into her eyes. "Tohni, I want you. All of you."

"Yes." She nodded and closed her eyes in ecstasy. "I want you too."

He kissed her lips with tender yearning and laid her back against the bean-bag chair, giving her a pillowed cushion. But at the moment she wouldn't have cared if they were in the middle of a rock pit; she only wanted him completely.

He hovered over her, his raging passion barely contained. Then there was no more holding back, for either of them. He slid between her thighs, hot burning flesh to hot burning flesh, his lips kissing her aching breasts, the pulsing column of her throat, her panting lips. She gasped with delight and surprise as he entered her, his tongue plunging between her teeth at the same time.

The motion of his brazen tongue matched

the movement of his pelvis and enticed her to join in the erotic dance. Savagely, the fire within them both raged higher and higher, creating a wild frenzy of uncontrolled passion.

Time stood still, preserving the glorious rapture between them. They clung together and dozed until the heat cooled and they were once again fully awake and aware. He nestled her in his arms, tucked her to his chest. With one leg wrapped securely over her hips he murmured sweet words.

"Oh, Tohni, to think we've denied ourselves this all this time."

"We were just too blind to look closer and see the real feelings."

"Too stubborn."

They cuddled quietly for a while. Finally Reese broke the silence. "I'm sorry I worried you today, but—in a way—I'm glad."

She smiled, pressing against the warm security of his chest. "It was worth it all, Reese, to end up in your arms. I realized today how much I care. I was so scared."

He caressed her back, running his fingers all the way down her spine, then resting them on the swell of her buttocks. "I never did tell you where I was." He chuckled.

"You don't have to tell me. I . . . have no ties on you."

Oh, yes, you do, little one. "I was only a block away in the park. With Vera Lee."

"With who? My mother?" She uncurled to look at his face. "You were with Mama?"

"Yes." He chuckled again. "We went to the park."

"What for?"

"To talk."

"About what?" Tohni was curious about Vera Lee's strange visit. "Mama was here? In this house? Then she knows about you living here?"

"Yes, Tohni. She's known all along. Only she thinks things have been different with us."

"More intimate?"

"Yes. I didn't disillusion her."

"Why bother?" Tohni grinned. "Well, what did she say?"

Reese assumed a mock-serious expression, but his eyes danced. "She asked, 'Since you two are living together, what are your intentions toward my daughter, Mr. Kreuger?'"

"Reese! She wouldn't say that," Tohni scoffed, then looked at him with a quizzical grin. "And? What did you tell her?"

"Well, I . . ." He cast devilish blue eyes at her. "Before I had a chance to tell her my true intentions, she invited us over for supper tomorrow night. I said great, since your daughter isn't the best cook in the world and I'm going stir-crazy in this apartment. So, okay? Do we have anything planned for tomorrow night? You might want to check the social calendar and make sure it's clear."

"Is that all? She came all the way over here from Decatur to invite us to supper."

"Well, she was probably in the neighborhood." He shrugged.

"That doesn't make sense. She's never in this neighborhood. It's too far away from hers. And not quite in the same class."

"Stella's fixing fried chicken and Waldorf salad. And pickled artichoke hearts and okra."

"Reese, I don't care what she's fixing for supper. What did my mother really want?"

"I'll never tell."

"Ah-ha! There *was* something else!"

"Tohni, my curious little private eye, our conversation was confidential. You don't want me to breach her confidence, do you?"

"She's *my* mother! What in the world would she say to *you* in confidence? And not to me? Tell me, Reese!"

"Not a chance." He chuckled and pressed her closer. "She'll tell you. In time. Right now, though, I'd rather hold you."

She wrapped her arms around his waist and whispered sexy words into his ear, feeling the pulse in his neck. She followed the regular throbbing with her lips, allowing her tongue to play against the pressure. "Love me . . ."

Gently he pulled her over him, kissing and teasing and touching in an unhurried, more complete game of love. They exchanged caresses and laughter. They explored and experienced and enjoyed. She kissed him, everywhere, then he laughingly rolled her over and proceeded to torment her with his tongue.

Finally, with leisurely precision, their bodies

210

merged in a different spirit of emotions. To-night was the beginning of a new sharing. Not just a blending of ideas and work. But of love. Or something close to it.

As Reese surged fully into her again, Tohni met his force with her own deep longing. Her heart swelled with love for him, for this man who showed love with his body but was unable to express it in words. Or unwilling. Yet she could tell, she could feel his love. It was strong and unyielding, like Reese himself.

Tohni was positive now of her love for him. She could only hope for Reese's love in return. In time.

In another part of Atlanta, two men worked late. The view of the city from the lofty office on Peachtree Street was magnificent. Yet neither man noticed.

The one with the large diamond ring spoke first. "I don't like the idea that Kreuger skipped out of the hospital so soon. Wasn't he injured pretty badly?"

"Broken arm and ribs. Nose too, I think. Lots of bruises."

"Hell, that should have kept him there for days. Where did he go anyway?"

"Don't know. Someone checked him out of the hospital, then came back to pay the bill."

"Who?"

"We couldn't find out."

"Hell, Jacoby! Can't you find out anything?

Who checked him out of the hospital? And where is he? Who's hiding him?"

Jacoby shook his head. "It's crazy. He's just disappeared. We're watching his apartment, and several friends'. And someone in Miami is keeping an eye on his family's home. He isn't anywhere to be found."

"I'm not satisfied with that answer. I want to talk to him again. Make sure he knows my position and that he intends to keep quiet. Find him."

"You mean, get the private eye again?"

"If that's what it takes, yes. I don't like it when somebody gives me the slip. This is twice now. I'm not a happy man, Jacoby."

"Yessir. We'll keep you happy." He left the room quietly, so as not to disturb the boss further.

Ansel turned to the mahogany chest behind his desk and extracted a bottle. He poured two fingers of Scotch and downed the fiery amber liquid in one large gulp. He drummed his fingers on the expensive oak desk.

"Damn Reese Kreuger anyway," he muttered. "How can one man make my life so miserable? Where can he have gone this time?"

CHAPTER THIRTEEN

"Why did you invite Joe tonight?" Tohni wanted to demand of her mother. But there wasn't time to pull her aside. Vera Lee was too busy being the perfect hostess.

They were an incongruous little group gathered around Vera Lee's expensive china- and crystal-laden dinner table. It was enough for Tohni and Reese to have to face her mother and try to reach some understanding about their living together. But that was a family affair. Why in the world had Vera Lee included Joe?

She had explained, as she swept the door open for Joe, that she wanted them all to get to know each other. But why? Tohni didn't even think her mother knew Joe except in passing. Oh, they had participated in a couple of flower shows together—horticultural competitions, Joe called them—but that hardly made them friends.

And since Joe and Reese had been cat-and-mouse adversaries, they would seem unlikely allies. Yet as Tohni picked at her Waldorf salad, the two men were engrossed in a conversation on the merits of a biodegradable fertilizer for roses. Amazingly enough, they'd been quite friendly all evening.

When Reese began to talk about his latest contact with the EPA and how he and Tohni had been busy preparing documents for the meeting, she realized that her mother had set this evening up for a reason. That's probably why she had dropped by the apartment yesterday. Another clue was that Joe hadn't been a raging bull when he saw her and Reese together. He'd been previously warned. So, for that matter, had Reese.

But what was Vera Lee's purpose exactly?

"It's so beautiful and warm tonight, we'll take our coffee and dessert out on the patio by the pool, Stella," Vera Lee said, signaling dinner's end.

Tohni jumped up, grateful for a chance to escape the confining walls of the dining room. "That's a great idea. I'll help you, Stella." She grabbed her empty plate and Reese's and disappeared into the kitchen. While the others ambled out to the patio, she cornered Stella.

"What's going on here, Stella?"

"I don't know what you mean, Miss Tohni."

"Don't give me that innocent look, Stella," Tohni hissed. "You do too."

"Only that Miss Vera has been seeing Mr. Staci occasionally."

Tohni screwed up her face and comically

placed her hands over her heart. "Joe? And my mother?"

"Hush, now," Stella warned. "Are you going to help me with these coffee cups? Or do you want to take the cherry cobbler?"

"I'll take the coffee." Tohni shook her head in disbelief. "I can't imagine it. Joe just isn't my mother's type."

"I don't know. Seems like a very nice man to me, Miss Tohni."

"Oh, he's nice. He just isn't rich." Tohni followed Stella's substantial bulk, with exquisitely thin china cups and a silver coffeepot loaded on the silver serving tray.

"Shhh," warned Stella as they reached the door.

"Must be platonic," Tohni muttered through her teeth. "It couldn't be anything else."

Vera Lee smiled generously as they approached. "Thank you, Stella. Everything looks beautiful. Tohni, how nice of you to help."

Tohni smiled tightly and set the tray on the glass-topped patio table. She arranged the cups and performed her social duty by pouring coffee from the silver pot without spilling a drop. They ate the crusty cobbler in relative silence and had refills of steaming hot coffee all around.

Finally, Joe broke the growing uneasiness. "Reese and Tohni, I think we'd better talk openly."

Uh-oh, thought Tohni. Here it comes. "This

215

isn't one of those what-are-your-intentions lectures, is it, Joe?"

Vera Lee fumbled with her napkin and stammered, "W-why Tohni dear, of-of course not."

"Oh, good. I always felt that was your area, Mama. And, actually, at my age, it isn't any of your business. Or yours, Joe."

Joe bulldozed his way back into the conversation. "Uh, Tohni, do you mind if I finish? I don't give a damn about your private life, except where it concerns my business. I've known for some time that you two were, uh, involved. And damn it, living together is involved!

"In fact, I guess I've known Tohni was interested in you, Reese, from the beginning, way back when she was reporting in from Tennessee." He paused to sigh heavily and shake his head. "Now, though, other things have come up to complicate matters, and I felt I should talk to both of you together. Vera Lee suggested we do it this evening."

Tohni gave her mother a quick, accusing look. "I knew something was up tonight. What's going on here?"

"Now, Tohni, sugar," Vera Lee soothed. "Just listen to Joe."

Joe stood up and began to pace the patio. "Reese, Tohni can tell you that I've always advised against any of my operatives getting involved in any way with subjects. It has nothing to do with individuals. It's policy. It's bad for business. Real bad. And bad for the operatives, uh, my employees. People like Tohni. Now I've never been in favor of this involvement you two have, but I've been ignoring it. I can ignore it no longer.

"When you got beaten up, Reese, I'll admit I became concerned about my part in all this. And when Tohni started playing her little games with me, I rebelled because I knew she wasn't following my orders. However, because of, uh, additional circumstances, I had to look at your situation differently."

"So what are you trying to say, Joe?" Tohni asked impatiently.

"I'm getting to it, Tohni." He ran an anxious hand through his hair, ruffling it a bit. Casting a quick glance at Vera Lee, he continued. "Reese, I got a call yesterday from Cornell Ansel. They're looking for you again. And it puts me in a bind, because of Tohni and you. Normally, I wouldn't hesitate to pick up a trail again. But this time it's different, and I thought I'd better tell you."

Reese nodded shortly. "I appreciate your honesty. What'd you tell him?"

"That all my operatives were tagged right now and I couldn't take it on. But I said I'd call him in a few days. I figured that would stall the action long enough for some decisions to be made."

"I knew it!" Tohni exploded. "I knew they'd be after him again! They won't stop until—" She pressed her fingers to her lips. "Well, we

217

aren't doing it, Joe. Why didn't you just give them a flat *no?*"

Joe ignored her outburst and directed his appeal to Reese, who was obviously more rational. "The reason I'm telling you all this is that I care about what you're doing. I know it's important to the welfare of everyone. But, Reese, these men are damned dangerous."

"Yes, I know they are. I've just spent several weeks thinking about how dangerous they are."

"Then listen to me," Joe urged. "Let it drop for now. At least for a couple of years until the subject cools down. Right now it's just too hot. By then Ansel will be thinking about other issues."

"A couple of years? *No!*"

The word exploded from Tohni's mouth, and everyone turned to look at her.

She leaned forward earnestly. "Don't you understand, Joe? The things Reese knows about this company are crucial to the health and welfare of thousands of people who live in the disposal areas. We're talking about something vital to life, not just here but all over the country."

"Tohni's right," Reese confirmed. "I can't stop now. I won't. I'll just have to deal with Ansel in whatever way is necessary. But I won't drop it. I can't. I've come too far now."

"I'm only suggesting this for your own safety, Reese," Joe hurried to add. "If you refuse to drop it, then I would advise you go into hiding

218

somewhere else until your reports have been filed with the EPA. And Ansel has been stopped. If not, you may be in serious danger for a long, long time."

"I know," Reese answered quietly. "But if I quit now, Ansel will have free reign to do whatever he wants wherever he can get away with it. There's no telling the amount of damage that'll be done. It's been going on too long now. For too many years. We have to put a stop to Ansel's midnight dumping. And get some regulations for toxic disposal that we, and future generations, can live with."

"I couldn't agree with you more. But we're talking about more than issues here, Reese. We're talking about people. There's . . . your life. And Tohni's."

"I realize that and I'm very concerned about her."

Joe sat down and faced Tohni. "Do you understand what we're saying, Tohni? Reese is in great danger. And if he continues this pursuit he'll always be on somebody's hit list. And if you're with him, so will you. For your mother's sake, I'm asking you to turn loose. Let Reese go his way until this thing is over."

"But you just said it may never be over." She blinked with the realization of what he was saying. "Hit list?"

"Things will change in time. So will people."

"And people's feelings?"

Joe nodded silently.

"No, Joe." Her voice was steady and firm. "I

can't. I've come this far with Reese, I want to go all the way. I'm convinced that what he's doing is right. And I want to help him bring it to a conclusion."

"Tohni, do you understand what you're saying?"

She slipped her hand into Reese's. "I'm standing with him on this, Joe. Mama, I only hope you understand. If you could read some of the reports I've been typing and knew the dangers of these chemicals, you would agree that too many people have kept quiet for too long."

"I hate to hear that, Tohni." Joe sighed heavily. "Because it means that I'll have to let you go."

There was a full minute of dead silence as it began to sink in that Tohni had just been fired.

Joe's voice was a low drone. "I couldn't let you continue working too long on a job that had even some normal degree of risk. And now you've placed yourself and your co-workers in far greater jeopardy. It's for your own good, Tohni, and for my other employees that I have to do this."

Tohni's gray eyes met Joe's defiantly and she blurted out, "You go to hell, Joe." Her hand flew to her mouth. She couldn't believe she'd said that to her boss. Her *former* boss.

"Tohni, he's right." Reese turned to her with a worried frown. "I can't let you do this. There's no need for you to ruin your life and lose your job over this. It's my problem, not yours."

"This problem is everyone's! That's what you say when you speak to groups. That's what you believe, Reese Kreuger! And it's what I believe!" Her gray eyes narrowed defiantly. "Whatever you do is my concern, Reese. I can't leave you now. I want to stay with you. It's the least I can do. Don't you know that by now?"

"Staying with me will not be easy, Tohni. I have to leave town and go into hiding again. I need to finish some jobs in Chattanooga. And I've already set up an appointment with the EPA office in Birmingham to present a preliminary report on Ansel. Who knows where we'll go from there."

"I'll go with you," Tohni vowed.

Vera Lee spoke up for the first time. "Reese, I feel you have a noble cause here and I'm in favor of your endeavors. The fact that my daughter has chosen to travel this perilous path with you is . . . unfortunate. But I won't stand in your way. Or hers. I have a friend in Chattanooga who would be absolutely delighted to hide you two away until you finish your business. She has plenty of room and would love the idea of your being in hiding. She's always had a flair for theatrics anyway."

"Mama, thanks." Tohni flashed Vera Lee a smile of amazement. Just when she'd thought her mother would cause problems, she came through with help.

Vera Lee smiled sweetly, almost innocently.

And yet she was contributing to a very dangerous plan. "You remember Arlene, don't you, sugar? She lives in that big house on Lookout Mountain."

Tohni nodded. "It's called a mansion in most circles, Mama."

Joe cleared his throat. "Uh, if Ansel should call back soon, I'll try to stall him and give you two time to get away. But, Tohni, you understand why I have to do this, don't you?"

"Yeah, Joe. It hurts you worse than me. It's been a long time since I've heard that speech. I think I was in high school, being subjected to restrictions for making a poor grade in chemistry."

Joe gave her a pleading look. "Tohni—"

She turned her head away in disgust. "Don't bother with any more explanations, Joe. I don't want to hear anymore. It's enough that you warned Reese and gave him a chance to get out of town. I'm extremely grateful for that."

Joe rose and walked away from the table, frustration written in every taut line of his face. He'd just fired his best operative. And sent her off on a trail of great danger. What if she gets hurt? What if Ansel's men catch up with them? What if . . . worse? Could he live with himself? Could he face Vera Lee? And yet he couldn't do a damn thing about it. It was Tohni's decision to follow Reese. And the damndest part about it was that, morally, they were right.

Vera Lee followed Joe into the dark shadows past the edge of the patio.

Reese turned to Tohni. "You've just screwed up your whole life because of me. Are you crazy?"

"What do I have to do to convince you my life would be screwed up without you, Reese Kreuger? We have something very important to do. Now let's get on with it. Those are my reports too. I put a lot of effort into writing and typing them. Plus, as you said once, you're right about this one. I believe it with all my heart." It was more than the effort that had gone into the reports, more than what was right or wrong. But Tohni couldn't say it. Not now. Maybe never, if Reese didn't share her feelings.

She turned to gaze defiantly at her mother and Joe, who stood in the rose garden across the backyard. In the shadowy light Tohni could see Vera Lee lift Joe's mitt of a hand to her lips.

For an instant Tohni's head whirled with anger and confusion. What was happening here tonight? Everything that had been steady and stable in her life was changing. Just when she thought her relationship with Reese was starting to grow, their world was going completely awry again. She'd lost her job. They would have to leave soon. Maybe tonight. And Reese was in danger again!

Now she knew why Joe had been invited. He was supposed to do the dirty work.

CHAPTER FOURTEEN

"Where the hell is Kreuger now?"

"We don't know, sir. We think he skipped town again."

"Where would he go? Did he go back to Tennessee?"

"It's possible. There were some unfinished jobs that were delayed by his, uh, unfortunate accident. He has contractual obligations with the University of Tennessee in Chattanooga, Mendal Manufacturing, and Hobbs Chemical."

Cornell Ansel paced before a glass wall that looked out over Atlanta. He concentrated on the situation, unconsciously jiggling change in his pocket. The jiggling stopped and he gave his assistant a hard glare. "I want him stopped before he does us any more damage. Is Eagle Eye still stalling?"

"Yessir. I talked to the boss today. He claims his staff has been reduced and he can't get to it until the weekend."

Ansel's eyes narrowed. "Jacoby, I don't give a damn about his internal problems. I only care about ours. And Reese Kreuger is number one on my list of problems. Find him! Shut him up! If Eagle Eye won't do it, find someone else who will."

"Yessir."

Latin bongo music surged from a small speaker cleverly hidden in a tree near the pool. Arlene's mansion and the surrounding yards were entirely walled in, providing the perfect hideout for Tohni and Reese. It was as if they were tucked away in their own little world atop Lookout Mountain. In Tohni's imagination the idyll of the last few days had been almost like a honeymoon. Almost.

"Now this is what I call living." Reese surrendered his lean swimsuited body to the padded lounger beside the pool and folded his hands beneath his tawny head. He turned his face up to receive the sun's full, hot blessing.

Tohni smiled happily at the relaxed golden body stretched out next to hers. Thank God, he had completely recuperated from his injuries. His face didn't show the bruises or swollen lumps anymore. But the broken bones had left their marks.

The face that she had once considered unrivaled was no longer perfect. His nose bore a slight bump to one side of the bridge and his left arm still wasn't quite as strong as the right. While his looks were no longer flawless, the faults seemed to make him even more attractive. More rugged. Of course, she viewed him entirely differently now than she had when spying on him through binoculars from the top of a hickory tree. Her perspective, admittedly, was biased by love.

Yes, love. She knew her feelings for Reese were deep, perhaps too deep for her own good. She knew it that night at her mother's when she told Joe to go to hell. She'd give up her job, her home, anything, for Reese Kreuger. Because he meant that much to her.

She could always find another job. But Reese was a man too special for words. And she didn't intend to lose him. She'd stay with him and help him and even fight for him if necessary. She'd fight in any way he needed. He hadn't the slightest suspicion of it, of course, but she'd even brought along her tiny purse revolver.

In fact, that was her main objective in tagging along on this trip. To protect him. Of course she'd only told him she wanted to help him file his reports. She pretended to be teasing when she claimed she was still his bodyguard. Actually, she was there for just that, to keep watch over their shoulders and around every corner. But this was the part she liked best: watching Reese relax.

Then Tohni closed her eyes too. "I could lie right here all day," she murmured.

"You promised me a game of tennis."

"Later. Can't you relax ten minutes?"

"That's all I've done for weeks," he grumbled.

"Is not. You worked."

"In my gilded cage."

"Are you complaining? At least you had a gym at your disposal. And me for company."

"Ah, yes. Such stimulating company! In more ways than one!"

"I'll take credit for that," she said with a laugh. "And consider it a compliment."

"Are you fishing for praise?"

"Heavens, no. We who are truly accomplished do not need mindless praise. Simple adulation will do nicely."

He leaned over and placed a kiss on the exposed swell of one breast. "How about if I admit that you turn me on when I see you in that itty-bitty pink bikini?"

"Please, dahling, be discreet. The hired help shouldn't see us like this."

"Then the hired help shouldn't look. Hell, I can't tell where that pink suit ends and your skin begins. Only by touch."

"And you managed to do that quite often, even in your gilded cage."

"Well, there wasn't much else for a body to do." He sighed.

"Are you insinuating that my presence merely kept you from being bored."

"My darling little spitfire, I would never say a thing like that. Of course you were more than that. Look at all the work we did."

"And don't forget it either, buster," she groused. "I've never typed so much in my entire life. My fingers are still sore."

"You did a stalwart if not entirely accurate job too."

"I warned you that typing is not my forte."

"I'll agree with that," he admitted. "You're much better at karate, my dear. Or creating a foolproof disguise."

"And don't forget the bodyguarding," she added.

"Heavens, no. Can't forget the bodyguarding. That's probably where you excel. And I can't complain about this plush week in Tennessee. The best I could come up with was a shabby little cabin on Lake Chickamauga. This mansion is fabulous! Vera Lee's friend Arlene certainly knew how to build a house, didn't she?"

"Given enough money, anyone could become quite creative, dahling," Tohni drawled with a grin. "This is just a little something she threw together to keep her kids off the streets."

"Tennis courts, swimming pool, shuffleboard court, game room complete with pool table, not to mention the baby grand piano in the music room. Should be enough to keep them occupied from toddlerhood into their golden years."

"Something to keep us occupied every day of the week for sure," Tohni agreed. "Too bad we have to work."

"Spoken from the heart of someone who just lost her job a few days ago," he quipped. "Incidently, you're quite cheerful considering you've been canned. That means no more pay checks, in case it hasn't settled in on you yet."

"Who needs money?" Tohni scoffed, and took another sip of her Seven-Up. "As long as my mother has rich friends like Arlene, we can just make the rounds from one to the other."

"You make it sound so easy. The free ride has to end sometime. And soon if I have anything to say about it."

"Spoilsport." She turned on her side and urged seriously, "Not yet, Reese. We've been here less than a week. And it's been so wonderful with just the two of us. Even though you've had to work, our free time has been great." *Our free and wonderful time together has been heavenly!*

"I know. Sorry to spoil your fun, but we do have an appointment next Monday with Michael O'Hara, the EPA's regional director in Birmingham. He can't see me sooner because he's on vacation." Reese gestured futilely in the air. "So while Mr. O'Hara is tanning his backside on Florida's shores or taking his kids to Disney World, Ansel is dumping illegally somewhere in Idaho."

"Take it easy, Reese. After all this time, what's one more week?"

Reluctantly he agreed. "Aw, you're right. What good will it do to work myself up about it? It's just that now I'm ready. The reports are satisfactory, and I don't look like a victim of a gang war. But still I have to wait."

"You won't be a victim again, Reese. Not if I have anything to do with it." There was a toughness in her voice and she meant every word. She intended to do whatever was necessary to keep him safe. "You still up for that game of tennis?"

He sat up. "Yeah. Sounds great. But I warn you, I was junior tennis champ the year before I started high school. And discovered girls. After that my tennis game went to hell."

"I warn you," she countered with grim determination, "I'm hell with a racket. And I hate to lose."

"If you play tennis anything like you execute karate moves, pip-squeak, I don't have a snowball's chance in hell! But the fun is in trying! Race you to the guesthouse!"

Shrieking with delight, she took off after him.

The sun was high in the clear blue sky above Lookout Mountain, and Reese was ahead forty–love in the fourth game of the second set when Tohni called him to the net.

"What do you mean, time to call it quits? Just when I'm ahead!"

"I've had enough. Let's go get something to drink."

"You aren't just being a sore loser, are you?"

"Damn it, Reese, don't argue with me. Someone's been watching us for the last hour and I feel uneasy. Let's go."

Reese swung around. "Who? Where?"

"Don't look!" she warned. "Just walk away slowly."

"Where is he? Or is it a woman?"

"A man, I think," Tohni explained in a low

voice. "He's on the other side of that wire fence across the yard. In the car parked across the street beneath those trees, with a pair of binoculars trained on us. Come on, Reese. Move slowly and act natural." She started to walk off the court.

"How did you see him? I didn't even notice that car and could have stared at it all day and not detected those binoculars."

Her mouth was tight. "That's what I'm trained for, remember? To be super observant."

"Well, you certainly are. I couldn't have picked a better bodyguard. Who do you think it is?"

"Either Joe has somebody watching us, or Ansel has hired someone else. Until we find out which, let's give him the slip."

"How do you propose to do that?"

"Follow me." Tohni casually propped her tennis racket against the fence and disappeared behind the bathhouse. Reese followed suit.

Behind the bathhouse was another fence. Tohni climbed to the top and jumped over. She glanced back and saw that Reese was following with little effort. After all he was taller and had spent hours staying in shape in the gym. Such activity was relatively easy for him.

They slipped the back way into Arlene's garage and drove out in her beige Mercedes.

"I'll have to talk to her about leaving keys in

231

her car," Tohni muttered. "This was just too easy."

"But it was in her own garage. Surely you can expect things to be safe on your own property."

Tohni shrugged. "Obviously not. See how easy it was for us to take it?"

"Not everyone has friends who steal their cars," Reese commented drily. "Anyway, it would've been just a healthier challenge for you if it had been locked up. I can remember one night a little curly-haired cat burglar slipping into my cabin by the lake. And I know the place was locked tight."

Tohni gunned the motor and drove rapidly through the narrow, winding residential streets of Lookout Mountain. "This is different. Arlene doesn't realize how easy she's made it for anyone to go into her garage and take her car. Anyway, I'm not going to steal it. We'll just borrow it for a while. If it's necessary to abandon it, I'll leave it in a safe place and call her."

"You sound like we might not come back."

"Depends. We might not."

"But I have to, Tohni. I left my briefcase in the guesthouse. That's where all my information on Ansel is. I can't leave without it."

"Oh, damn! Well, let's get it now before we get too far away." She circled around and drove back to Arlene's mansion. Halting the Mercedes behind the guesthouse, she pointed out their nemesis, who had moved his car to another spot. "Look! He's still watching the

232

house. He thinks we'll be back. Mistake number one, jerk! We won't be back!" Motioning to Reese, she said, "I'll run in and get the briefcase. You stay hidden here, Reese. Duck down in the seat."

"You aren't expecting we'll return, then?" he asked.

"Probably not. It's too dangerous. You can tell it's what our tail expects us to do. So we'll have time to lose him before he realizes we're gone for good."

"Then get my billfold. And . . . anything else we might need."

"Sorry we don't have time to change clothes. I'll grab what I can though."

She darted through the back gate of the high-walled mansion. Within a few moments she was back with the briefcase and her purse in tow. "Now let's get out of here. Oh, no! He's spotted us!"

The next fifteen minutes were a wild game of hide-and-seek on the winding mountain roads curving through the residential sections of Lookout Mountain. Only someone who knew where he was going could drive the streets faster than twenty-five miles an hour and keep from pulling into a dead-end street. Someone like Tohni.

"I think I've lost him." She kept an eye on the rearview mirror.

"Now what?"

Tohni continued to drive, finally pulling to a stop at Point Lookout, a park filled with milling tourists. "Want an interesting ride, Reese? This might just work. Come with me."

They dashed inside a building, dressed in their tennis whites. It wasn't a very good disguise and they certainly didn't blend in with the tourists, but it couldn't be helped right then. Tohni pushed her way to the head of the line waiting for tickets.

Ignoring grumblings of "Rude!" and "Quit pushing!" she purchased two tickets and rushed through the small station which, Reese couldn't help but notice, was perched on the very edge of the mountain. They hopped aboard a waiting tram.

"Whoa!" Reese took a seat, then glanced out the window. The view was spectacular—straight down!

"We're going the scenic route," Tohni quipped as she kept a watchful eye on the crowd outside the window. "You can see all of Moccasin Bend from here." She pointed to where the Tennessee River curved around a section of earth with a bootlike shape.

"Yeah, real nice. I'll take the guided tour next trip, thanks." Reese watched anxiously as the little cable car started its descent. They traveled straight down to the very bottom of Lookout Mountain. "Has this thing ever come unhooked?" he asked anxiously.

"No." She laughed. "It's called the Incline. Goes all the way down to Saint Elmo. They've used this method of traveling the mountain as long as I can remember. We'll lose our tail for sure this way, especially if our man doesn't know the mountain very well. And apparently he doesn't."

"Saint Elmo? As in Saint Elmo's fire, strange lights in the night?"

"We might see some fire if we get caught! Actually, Saint Elmo's just a little suburb of Chattanooga." She clutched her purse tightly, reassured to know it contained a weapon she prayed she'd never have to use.

At the bottom of the mountain they again dashed among tourists. Quickly, Tohni found a pay phone and began feeding it quarters. "All your change please. You keep a watch for our man while I call Joe and see what's happening." Her fingers shook with anticipation as she punched the familiar numbers.

Reese leaned against the phone-booth door. "I'd be glad to contribute if I had any money. You didn't think to bring my billfold, did you?"

She gave him a smug smile and opened her large purse. "One man's billfold coming up."

He glanced into her purse, and his eye caught something else. A glimmer of the sun on a piece of metal. "Tohni! What the hell is that?"

She tried to close her purse, but he caught her hand. "Now, Reese, before you say a thing, I've been carrying this for years. It's just an element of my job."

"You've been fired, remember?" His blue eyes were cold glints. "I don't want any violence, Tohni."

"I don't want any *more* violence, Reese."

"Damn it, Tohni, I don't like this."

"Listen, Reese, I've never had to use it in five years of investigating and bulldogging."

"Don't think you're going to use it this time."

"Just in case, Reese. Reserve protection. Uh-oh, the phone's ringing." She turned her attention to the phone. "Joe? Do you have someone tailing us?"

"Tohni! How are you? And where?"

"Right now we're fine. But someone's on our tail. Is it one of your operatives?"

"Hell, no! I stalled them as long as I could. If someone's after you, Ansel must have hired another agency. Damn it, Tohni! Don't be a fool! If you're being followed, go to the police!"

"Oh, yeah, they'll love that. We're being followed by someone. Don't know who. Can't prove it, but I think I saw a car tailing us."

"Where are you?"

"We gave him the slip on the mountain. But, Joe, we can't go back to Arlene's. We need help. Someplace else to go."

"Oh, hell. Let me think."

"We need to be in Birmingham next week. Reese has an appointment with the EPA's regional director. But until then . . ."

"Birmingham, huh? Hiding out? Let me see now. Ah, here's the number. Take this number down, Tohni. He's an old friend of mine from army days. But I'll bet he can help you. His place is on the other side of town, around by

Moccasin Bend. It isn't very fancy, but you don't have much choice now."

"Anything, Joe. We're in a bind." Tohni scribbled furiously as Joe talked. "Okay. Thanks a million, Joe."

"Uh, Tohni? Can I call Vera Lee? Tell her you're okay?"

"Yeah, Joe. Tell her we're fine. Just fine."

"Okay, kid. Keep in touch."

"Thanks, Joe. And . . . Joe? I didn't mean to tell you to go to . . . uh, you know."

"Yeah, kid. I know. Remember everything I taught you. You're gonna need it. Have you got your piece?"

"Yes. But I . . . I've never used it, Joe."

"Don't worry about it. If you have to, you'll know when. And how."

"Okay." Her voice was soft. Joe was encouraging and caring, in his own gruff way.

"Good luck, kid."

"Thanks." She swallowed hard and faced Reese with a smile. "Okay. We're all set. I'll explain on the way. But first we have to make a stop at a used-clothes store. I think I spotted one down the street. These tennis clothes will not do where we're going. Maybe we can work a swap."

"Where're we headed now, Tohni?"

"Stick with me, kid, and I'll take you places." She grinned. "And keep you safe. I'm your bodyguard, remember?"

CHAPTER FIFTEEN

They walked the plank behind Homer Dickens. The plank, a weathered gray walkway, led from the pier to a sleek wood-and-glass houseboat. Reese blended in with his blue-gray overalls, a navy shirt, and white tennis shoes, despite his valuable briefcase. Not too conspicuous. Tohni's overalls were even more faded and she'd had to roll up the legs because they were too long. She had even managed to find an old frayed straw hat in the back of the used-clothing store. She looked like a character straight out of *Huckleberry Finn*. All she needed was a piece of straw to chew on.

"Any friend of Joe Staci's is a friend of mine. How's that old sonavagun anyway?" Homer asked.

"He's fine," Tohni said, glancing skeptically at the houseboat. "Just fine."

"Last I heard he was with the DA's office in Atlanta. Always thought he'd end up in politics. In the mayor's office or something. He was always a great one for words. Persuasive, you know?"

Tohni looked surprised. This was a side of Joe she'd never noticed. "Joe, in politics? Heavens, no. He has his own business."

"Eh? What kind of business?"

"Private investigations. Is this the kitchen?"

"Yep. In here's the kitchen. Beds are to the back." Homer scratched his head. "You mean Joe's doing stuff like on those shows we see on television? Chasing criminals and solving crimes?"

"Yeah. Something like that." Tohni nodded absently.

"Does he carry a gun too?"

"Gun? Huh? Oh, sometimes. Very rarely though. He, uh, has a permit to carry one if necessary. Well, thank you very much, Mr. Dickens," Tohni said, trying to end the conversation so they could be on their way. She thought of the gun she had hidden in the bottom of her purse and how rarely she had occasion to carry it. Like, never. Until now. But she, too, had a permit to use it, if necessary.

Reese had entered the covered part of the houseboat and was poking around the living area. He stashed his briefcase before returning to the porch that surrounded the cabin.

Homer showed them the control console, a rather modern steering apparatus with gauges, steering wheel, and throttle all within an arm's reach. He seemed to enjoy their company and was in no hurry to see them depart. "Yeah, lots of folks are renting these houseboats nowadays. It's funny. When I was a kid we lived on the

239

river because we couldn't afford anything else. 'Course, our house didn't look anything like this one. Now, though, folks do it just for fun. Why, with this newfangled Tombigbee Waterway that connects the Tennessee River to the Mississippi, a person could go all the way down to New Orleans." Homer chuckled. " 'Course, you'd have to go through a number of lock and dams, but some do it."

"We don't need to go as far as New Orleans, Mr. Dickens. We'd like to go to Birmingham though."

"The closest you could get is Guntersville, Alabama. You'll have to go through the lock at Nickajack Dam, but that shouldn't cause you too much trouble."

"Guntersville, huh?" Tohni did some quick figuring. "Could we leave the houseboat there, Mr. Dickens? We have some business down there and I don't think we'll have time to return it here."

Homer Dickens looked at her askance. "We-e-ll, I don't know about that, lady. . . ."

Reese stepped forward and handed Homer a hundred-dollar bill. "Perhaps it would be okay if we paid you for your trouble? Also, to keep quiet if anyone asks about us."

"Why, sure, mister." Homer grinned slowly and took the bill. "You two aren't in any trouble with the law, are you?"

"Oh, no," Tohni chimed in, showing Homer her agent's badge. "We're on a special assignment for Joe. It's high-level security and very

240

secretive. We're depending on you to help us until we've solved this case."

"Oh. Well, that's different. I'd be glad to help." Homer nodded eagerly and tucked the bill into the bib pocket of his overall.

"Thanks for being so helpful and cooperative, Mr. Dickens," Reese said, extending his hand to shake. "We'll tell Joe what a help you were. Maybe we can get you a commendation or something."

"That's mighty fine of you, mister. Hope you two have a good time on the river. Tell old Joe I said hello next time you see him."

"We'll tell him. And thanks." Tohni waved and Reese started the motor. Homer had hardly lifted the plank when they set off on their river journey.

"Reese, do you think this'll be okay?" Tohni slipped into his arms as he steered the boat.

"Sure. Like Homer said, people do this every day just for fun."

"Do you think it's safe?"

"I think it's a fabulous idea. Who would ever think to look for us on the river? And if they do, I believe Homer'll keep quiet. He seems to be a man of his word."

Tohni sighed. "Then let's try to enjoy it and forget about the meeting next week and the people chasing us. I don't want to think about it until we have to."

His lips nibbled at her ear. "This is going to be great, Tohni. Boats appeal to me anyway. After all, we had our first date on a boat."

241

"Date? I'd hardly call that a date."

"Well, there were lots of firsts that day."

She smiled up at him. "I think I'm going to like this, Reese."

Before long Tohni and Reese grew to appreciate the wild and free spirit of the houseboat. Their world consisted of just the two of them, floating through life and viewing activity along the river banks. They could stop long enough to watch or take part if they wanted to, and continue on their journey when they grew restless. Around the bend there was always another sight to see, another world to experience.

But what they both loved most about the trip was that it threw them totally and completely together. Just the two of them. The real world existed only at a distance. It was wonderful.

They docked nights at small, out-of-the-way piers attached to small, out-of-the-way settlements. Sometimes there was a grocery store for food, other times they simply caught fish for supper. Life was simple and uncomplicated. And the danger that had surrounded them for weeks seemed far away.

But their time was limited. They spent the lazy time fishing or exploring remote coves. At night they lay in each other's arms and made love. Or they fell asleep with a deep, warm satisfaction simply because they were together.

Tohni wanted to stop the clock and make their week's idyll last forever. Or at least longer than one short week. The time flew by, and Tohni worried that this would be their last time together . . . alone. Yet she sensed that now was not the time to press Reese about the long-term chances of their relationship. Occasionally he seemed preoccupied and Tohni was sure he was thinking about the events that were upcoming. Once, out of the clear blue, he even said, "I'll be glad when this whole mess is over."

Tohni knew he meant the meeting with the EPA and his trouble with Ansel. But the date with the EPA would also mean the end of their journey. Perhaps even of their relationship. She didn't comment, just nodded in agreement.

She wondered what would happen to them when he no longer needed her. What would happen when they were no longer partners in this strange chase? Would Reese go back to Atlanta and more toxic-waste projects? Or would he move on, to another town and another life? And another love?

What would she do? Go to Joe and beg for her old job back? She only knew one thing. She would never love anyone as she loved Reese. The thought of another man taking his place repulsed her. The thought of losing him frightened her.

The night before they reached their destination Tohni couldn't sleep. A hundred thoughts chased around in her head until finally she slipped out of Reese's secure arms. Moonlight filtered through jalousie windows and softly bathed his golden masculine body.

Oh, how she loved him. He was so gorgeous, so handsome, even with the bump on his nose and the slightly crooked jaw. He was so committed, so brilliant, so damned honest. At that moment she wished she could persuade him to run away with her, to flee the country and forget this whole mess. But he wouldn't do that. She knew him too well even to dream about it.

Reese continued to sleep under her loving gaze. His noble head was thrown back, his face turned away from her, and it was all she could do to keep from combing that thatch of unruly sandy hair with her fingers. One arm was flung out over the pillow, as if reaching for her, the other folded across his chest, fingers curved over the soft mat of chest hair. Remembering the strength and skill of those fingers and how they felt as they touched her so thoroughly sent a heated flush over her.

Her eyes roamed lower, to the sheet tangled around his legs, barely covering the masculine bulge at the juncture of his long legs. He had the kind of body that a woman could admire shamelessly. She knew how much pleasure his body had given her and wondered how many other women had felt that same way. When all this was over, would there be another?

Disquieted by the thought, she moved outside on the porch to stare at the black water surrounding them. A cloud moved before the moon, sometimes blotting it completely, sometimes allowing a gleaming, rippling path of light to cross the black river. A lone whippoorwill broke the stillness of the night and an owl answered. Strange bedfellows, Tohni thought with a shiver, pulling a soft blanket tighter about her shoulders. She was nude beneath the blanket.

"I'll bet that lonely whippoorwill woke up to find his bed empty and cold."

Tohni started at his voice. "Reese. I didn't hear you come out here." They whispered, though neither knew why. Ostensibly they were alone. Still, they whispered.

"I didn't hear you leave. What's wrong, Tohni? Can't sleep?"

She nodded and opened the blanket to him. He moved his nude body next to hers, the two bare forms huddling together beneath the blanket.

"How can it be so hot during the day and cool enough for a blanket at night?" he murmured, wrapping an arm around her back.

She shrugged. "That's life on the river."

"I'll be sorry to see the end to our little river excursion."

"Me too."

"Is that what's keeping you awake?"

"I guess."

"Tohni, it'll be okay. We'll work things out—"

"Don't, Reese. We started out with no commitments, remember? There's no need to start now. Not now."

He breathed steadily for a few moments. "Tohni, surely you know I've loved every minute we've been together. Well, almost all. But this meeting with O'Hara, and the possible consequences, are weighing on my mind. Everything I've worked for centers around it. After that we can concentrate on us."

"I understand, Reese. In a few days we'll have time to decide what all this means."

"Tohni, Tohni, what would I do without you?" He pulled her to him and kissed her long and hard. His knee moved naturally between her thighs and pressed against the sweet juncture of her legs. Their bodies seemed to reach out as they shifted positions, trying to get closer.

Unexpectedly, a noise on shore grabbed their attention. The sound wasn't like any of the river sounds they'd grown used to during the past week. It was metal hitting metal. Tohni's first thought was of a gun.

"What was that?"

"Don't know." Reese sucked in his breath. "Listen. Look."

They both strained their ears and eyes in the darkness, made more opaque by the cloud covering the moon at that instant. Then they dropped down, lying almost flat on the deck.

Tohni's heartbeat tripped as she imagined a team of Ansel's men getting ready to storm their idyllic little houseboat. What would the men do? Whisk Reese away? Beat him? She remembered with chagrin that they were both nude and completely vulnerable. Dear God, she knew what they'd do to her!

But she had a defense! She still had her gun! Maybe if she fired it into the air, it would scare them away. Just as she was about to tell Reese she was going for the gun, he hissed in her ear.

"Look! A still!"

"Still? Oh, a whiskey still!" Tohni blinked at shadowy forms moving in the hazy moonlight. A small building and a contraption of pipes. A fire, barely visible.

If she and Reese hadn't been awake at that ungodly hour, if they hadn't heard the faint clinking noise, if they hadn't stared at that particular spot on shore, they would never have noticed a thing. They would never have seen the signs of illegal activity. Normally, no one would ever know. Normally. But she and Reese were now privy to this secret. Just as Reese had been privy to Ansel's secrets. What was it with them anyway? Couldn't they keep their noses out of trouble?

Tohni tried to block out the knowledge by squeezing her eyes shut. Then, overcome with giddy relief, she slumped against Reese. "They're only making white lightning. Thank God! I thought it was Ansel's men."

"Shh. We don't want them to know we've seen them."

"But, Reese, we'd never tell! We're certainly not going to get involved in this!"

"I'm in no condition to convince them of that," Reese mumbled. "Nor are you!"

"No, I guess not." She laughed, letting her hand trail along the hairy planes of his chest and down to his waist. And lower.

"Tohni, you're treading on dangerous territory."

"Good. I love the thrill of the chase."

"You won't have to chase long to arouse a thrill in me."

"Is that a promise?"

"Absolutely."

Keeping low, they crept back to the bedroom, out of sight of the moonshiners. When they reached the safety of the bed he pulled her to him, over him, molding her softness to his hard, muscular body. As his hands cupped her buttocks, widespread fingertips digging into the flesh, she moaned softly. He pressed and the firm ridge of his arousal could be felt against her belly. She slid her hand between them, her fingers surrounding him, stroking vigorously.

"I want you . . ." she murmured between kisses.

"Ah, you feel wonderful. Warm and . . . so good."

"Reese, make me yours tonight. Tonight and forever."

"Forever," he answered, and raised up to kiss her breasts, suckling hard on the nipples. "Oh, God, you're delicious."

She arched her small breasts to meet the sweet, warm velvet of his mouth. Oh, she loved his wild, wonderful sensuality, this extra delight he seemed to take in her small body. To-night, especially tonight, his caresses, his kisses, were heavenly.

"Beautiful . . . delicious . . ." he murmured as his tongue lapped the strawberry areoles that seemed to push themselves into his mouth. He rolled her over onto her back and proceeded to kiss every part of her. He pushed her arms above her head and watched appreciatively as the shape of her breasts changed. Then he stroked them with his tongue while she writhed with pleasure.

She gave herself freely, eagerly, delighting in his erotic machinations. When his hands sought her soft center of desire, the feminine petals opened to receive his gentle probing. She surged against the heel of his hand as his thumb caressed her tiny, hard bud of passion. Soft moans echoed in her throat as fiery streams shot through her veins, which threatened to burst if he didn't stop. Yet she would die if he withdrew right now.

"Reese . . . oh, don't stop . . . now . . . come to me."

Frantically, flooded with warmth and desire to the very core of her being, Tohni guided his aroused manhood to her.

Uttering a low groan, he was suddenly out of control. Like a wild man he thrust savagely into her. She accepted his power as an unspoken avowal of his love and met his desire with a fire of her own. This was something neither could resist, or control, from the moment they'd met. The spark of desire was there, a spark that had now grown to a brushfire consuming them both.

They rode higher and higher until they reached a dramatic, earth-shattering climax as one.

Tohni clasped him to her. "Reese, never leave me."

"I need you, Tohni. I'll always need you."

She fell asleep in his arms, praying that he would always need her. That they would always be together.

The next morning Tohni strained to see the moonshiners' still through the heavy Alabama foliage on shore. Trying as hard as she could, she couldn't spot it. She questioned whether they had even seen anything last night. Yes, damn it, they had seen it together. They had discussed it. Then they had gone inside to make love. Wild and wonderful love that blotted out the entire world.

She couldn't help wondering if Reese's vow to always need her would be forgotten and disappear in the light of day, the way the moonshiners' still had. Oh, she knew it was there. But it was carefully camouflaged. Was that the way it was with their love?

They docked the houseboat at Guntersville, and with pangs of remorse and sad, wistful smiles, abandoned their idyll. There was work to do. They rented a car and drove to Birmingham. The plan was to spend the night in a motel and find a place to purchase reasonable clothes for the EPA meeting the next day. Overalls simply wouldn't do.

The large, almost vulgar diamond glistened in the lamplight as Cornell Ansel made an unusual late night phone call in Atlanta. "Jacoby? Are you ready for action? I know where he is."

"They found Kreuger? Oh, hell! Did they find him in Tennessee?"

"No. But we know exactly where he'll be tomorrow at one o'clock."

"Where in hell is he?"

"Birmingham. Just got an interesting call from an inside source. He has a one o'clock appointment tomorrow with Mr. Michael O'Hara."

"The EPA head?"

"Yes. Needless to say, I don't want him to make that meeting, Jacoby."

"Yessir. We'll get right on it."

"Get our friends on their way. I want him to have a welcoming reception he'll never forget."

"Yes, Cornell."

"Why the hell did Kreuger think he could get away with this? He's trying to make a fool of me. Trying to ruin me! Damn him anyway! I'll show him who's in charge here. And what money will do."

"Ye—" The other phone clicked off and Jacoby held his phone for a moment before slamming it down.

CHAPTER SIXTEEN

"Is this part of your training?"

"What?"

They stood beside the elevator in the Federal Building. Reese was dressed in a conservative suit of powder gray with tiny pinstripes. Tohni was neatly attired in a navy suit with a tailored red blouse and narrow matching tie. To all appearances they were stable, no-nonsense types who were conscientious and principled concerning the accusations they were about to present to the district EPA office.

"Did your investigative training teach you how to come up with the appropriate clothes for any occasion? You seem to be able to dress up for anything."

"It's a special knack." She smiled. "Facilitated by the miracle of plastic money when all you own are a pair of well-worn overalls."

"How in the world did Sherlock Holmes carry out his investigations and ease himself out of unexpected spots before the golden age of credit cards?"

"Beats me." She shrugged and stepped with

Reese into the elevator. When the door closed and they were alone, she gave him an approving once-over. "Ve-ry nice. You must admit, you had to have new clothes. After all, you couldn't very well make a credible presentation to the EPA district manager in overalls."

"I'd prefer the gorilla suit." Reese checked his cuffs, feigning a snobbish air. "Frankly, I wish you'd worn your overalls. The way they fit your rear end is so cute." He bent over and kissed her nose, then straightened quickly as the elevator halted for more passengers.

Tohni sighed. It was almost over. Michael O'Hara of the EPA awaited them upstairs.

She noticed the two men who stepped aboard the elevator were extraordinarily tall. And big. After that things moved very swiftly.

The first man inserted a key in the elevator control panel, stopping it with the door shut. The largest man grabbed Reese, forcing both of his arms behind him. The briefcase dropped to the floor and Reese uttered a muffled grunt of pain.

At that moment Tohni sprang into action. Making a tight fist, she punched the thug who restrained Reese in the kidney as hard as she could. His groan assured her she'd hit her mark. When he loosened one arm on Reese, she grabbed it and tried to fold it behind him.

Reese broke loose and jabbed his assailant in the solar plexus. The man staggered against the wall with a groan.

The other hoodlum lunged and grabbed

Tohni by the hair. He buried his large hand in her dark curls as he yanked her against him and jabbed something that felt like steel into her ribs.

"Unless you want the little lady to die young, buddy, you'd better do as I say."

Everything halted in silence. Reese stopped mid-action. His hard blue eyes sought Tohni's, then he lowered them to her midsection. She was definitely in trouble!

The man held her firmly by a handful of hair and her expression told Reese she was in pain. But she didn't utter a sound. He detected a barely discernible nod affirming the threat was for real.

"I've got a gun to her ribs, buddy. If you want to see her make it outta here alive, you better calm down."

Reese lifted both hands. "Sure, sure. I'm calm. What do you want?"

"Get in that corner and stand still. Mort, you all right?" Obviously this one with the gun in his pocket, the one who spoke, was in charge.

Mort lunged at Reese. "You SOB! I'll work you over—"

Reese threw up his left arm to deflect the blow.

Tohni gasped as she realized that's probably how Reese's arm had been broken in the original assault. Oh, God, they were going to do it again! Not if she could get her hands on the gun in her purse though! Her mind raced with plans for making that possible.

"Damn it, Mort! Not here. Back off! We want him able to walk out of here! The girl's a different story."

"He knocked hell outta me! And that little bitch punches like a kangaroo! I'm gonna get 'em both!"

"Not now, Mort! We have a job to do. Specific instructions. You listen to me."

Mort gave the leader a sullen look but backed off.

"Now . . . you!" The leader gestured to Reese with the object in his pocket. "You walk straight ahead when this thing opens. Act like nothing happened. Don't look around. Don't try to warn anybody. Don't make a run for it. If you have plans like that, remember to bid your little girl friend bye-bye before we stop, because she won't be around long. You go straight through the lobby. There'll be a car waiting out front. Walk directly to it and get in. We'll be right behind you."

"I'll do what you say. But turn her loose!" Reese commanded desperately, his blue eyes revealing the fear he felt for Tohni.

"Shut up! When this door opens, you walk. Got that clear?"

"Look, she doesn't know anything about this. Leave her here. Ansel isn't after her." It was a frantic plea from Reese.

Mort objected vehemently. "Don't let her go! The little bitch hit me—and hard! I have a score to settle with her!"

"Both of you shut up and listen to me," the

first hoodlum shot back. "We are leaving this place. First, I'm going to release this elevator. Are you ready to do what I said?"

Mort nodded. "Go ahead." He moved closer to Reese and locked onto his elbow with a vise-like grip.

The leader released his grip on Tohni's hair and turned the key in the control panel. The elevator began to move. Tohni stood still, frozen in place. Fear raked through her. They were in a perilous situation and she dared not try to grab her gun now. She'd have to watch for a better time. But she was reassured just knowing it was there.

When the elevator door opened, Reese walked out first. Mort made a noise and clutched Reese's elbow. They stopped. "We forgot that case he was carrying. It's on the floor."

"Leave it," the leader barked. "Nobody said nothin' about bringing a briefcase."

"They didn't say nothin' about a girl either."

"Get goin'!"

They started again, all four marching through the lobby in very close proximity. When they reached the street, Reese was shoved into a black limousine and the others followed him in. The vehicle rolled away from the curb and into traffic.

Reese sat upright and motioned to Tohni. "Damn it! Why did you have to bring her along? She doesn't belong here!"

"Hey, buddy, my patience with you is runnin' out! Shut up! I'll decide who belongs here! Mort, get those strips."

Mort tied blindfolds on both Tohni and Reese and they sat in blackness and silence. Half an hour later they reached their destination and were jerked roughly out of the limo. Tohni clutched at her purse, but someone ripped it from her hands and threw it back on the seat.

"My purse—I need it!"

"Not where you're going, sister."

"It—it has my contacts."

"Get going! You won't need contacts either."

Tohni stumbled along, mad and frustrated. They now had her only recourse. Her gun! Damn! Damn! Damn!

The two thugs shoved Reese and Tohni down the basement stairs of an abandoned ramshackle apartment building on the south side of town. As they lay in rumpled heaps, their hands were jerked behind their backs and tied. Mort couldn't resist a final kick at Reese's back.

There was shuffling and the sound of a bolt locking into place. Then in the distance two men could be heard, and Tohni knew Mort wanted to work them over as he'd threatened. But the gruff leader said, "They'll get theirs. . . ." And the two men left.

Fear gripped Tohni, chilling her even in the heat of the day, for she knew someone would be back for them. Then what? They had to get out of here as soon as possible.

When everything was quiet, Reese said, "Tohni? Are you all right?" His voice was muffled and she knew he was probably in pain from the blows he'd received.

"Yes," she mumbled, and struggled to sit upright. They both still wore blindfolds and had been tossed around so much, it was difficult to get their bearings. "Reese, are you? Did they . . . did they hurt you?"

"No broken bones. I think I can work my hands loose. Then I'll get to yours and we'll see if we can get out of here."

What seemed at first like an easy task took Reese over an hour. When he'd finally worked his hands free he tore off his blindfold and scrambled to Tohni's side. Lifting her blindfold, he framed her face with numbed hands, then caressed her tousled hair. "Oh, God, Tohni, are you all right?" He kissed her face, her eyes, her lips. "I should never have brought you along. I got you into this mess, baby, and I'm sorry. I'll get you out. It'll be all right."

"Don't be silly. I wanted to help you and knew the risks involved. I'm all right. Just get me loose."

He turned her around and worked frantically at the ties binding her wrists. Finally, with the help of a rusty file found in a corner he managed to free her. With numbed hands they clung to each other frantically. Then Reese pushed her away to arm's length. "We have to get out of this place. Now."

"Damn it, Reese! They took my purse!"

"Don't worry about that now."

"It had my gun! That was our protection! Our only protection! And now it's gone!"

"It's only protection if you're willing—or able—to use it. And so far, you haven't been either."

"But I might have. I would have," she amended stoutly. "If I still had it."

"I doubt it."

"Reese—"

"Don't worry about the gun. It's gone. I doubt if either of us could have fired it at another human. And let's hope we won't ever have to make that decision."

She clamped her jaws with determination and didn't answer. He was probably right. The gun had done them no good in the elevator. But just having it in her purse had given her a feeling of security in the back of her mind.

They explored their small prison. It was an enclosed area with no windows and a single door that was bolted tight. Their captors had obviously picked a remote spot that could be secured easily, and it looked as if they were completely trapped.

The room was fairly empty except for a rusty old furnace in the corner. Apparently this had been the furnace room of the old apartment building. They found that the heat ducts from the furnace provided an exit. *The only way out!*

Systematically, they began to take the rusted pipes apart, working feverishly against time. It

259

was midafternoon and hot and stuffy. They discarded their once-neat suit jackets and continued to work, thoroughly drenched in perspiration. It didn't matter. They had to get out!

Finally, the last of the pipes was ripped away from the duct. "There!" Tohni said with satisfaction, then peered closer. "Ohmigod! Can you crawl through that opening, Reese? It's pretty small."

He studied the black tunnel. "I have to, Tohni. It's our only way out."

Reese led the way. On all fours they proceeded into the dark hole.

"Eek! What's that?" Tohni screeched as something furry touched her hand.

"Shh! Just a mouse."

"In a place like this it would have to be a rat! Oh, dear God! A rat!"

"It's gone. Come on!"

"Oh, Reese, I don't like this at all. There are probably spiders and everything in here! I don't think I can go much farther."

"Don't think about it. You can't stop now. Come on just a little farther. I see a speck of light. It isn't too much farther, Tohni." He continued his verbal encouragement all the way through the sooty tunnel. The space was so confining, his shoulders barely fit. He couldn't turn around and touch Tohni. He could only go forward and talk. So that's what he did.

At last they reached the end! They crawled into open space and found themselves on the second floor. Some of the walls and floors had caved in, and they had to pick their way carefully through the sunken hallways and down the stairs. They didn't realize how much time had elapsed as they'd concentrated on freeing themselves. It was dark when they finally jumped to the earth outside the building. And freedom!

They found themselves in a sleazy part of town and wandered around awhile before spotting a cab.

"Do you think it's safe to go back to our motel?" Tohni asked as Reese waved to the cabbie.

"I figure it's as safe as any place. They don't know where we're staying. That's why they met us in the Federal Building. Anyway you need a shower. You look like you've been crawling through heat ducts."

"You should see yourself." She sniffed and climbed into the cab. "You look like a chimney sweep."

Once inside the secure walls of their motel room Tohni and Reese looked at each other and burst into hysterical laughter. What a mess they were!

Both had forgotten their jackets back in the little furnace room. Tohni's skirt was no longer blue and her red blouse was covered with black soot. Her skirt was ripped to the thigh and the toes of her smart navy pumps were scuffed from crawling.

Reese's conservative powder-gray pants were now filthy and beyond repair, and the shoulders of his shirt were black and shredded where they'd scraped the top of the sooty ducts. The once-immaculate cuffs of his white shirt were frayed and jet-black. His slacks bore several rips, and one tanned knee showed through a large three-cornered tear.

Disregarding all that, they threw their dirty arms around each other and stayed that way for a long, long time. They didn't even bother to say how wonderful it was to be safe at last. And alive. But they felt it through and through, and expressed that feeling to each other by touching and occasionally releasing a deep sigh.

After a long hot shower, Reese sent out for sandwiches and a bottle of wine. Afterward they fell into bed, wrapped in each other's arms, clinging together like that, safely, all night long.

Tohni awoke alone the next morning.

She bounded out of bed, panicked that Reese was gone. Crazily, she thought someone had abducted him for his clothes were gone too. She couldn't believe he'd willingly wear those dirty, sooty clothes he'd dropped on the floor last night. She figured they were good only for burning. Was he that desperate to leave? Or was he forced to?

Then she saw the note lying on the dresser. One of his credit cards lay nearby.

Darling, Use my card to fly back to Atlanta. I'll meet you there when this mess is all over. I don't want you hurt. I love you, Reese.

Her hand shook.

Tears sprang to her eyes.

She gasped for air.

Love! Love?

For how long had she wanted to hear him say that word? How many times had she been tempted to wake him in the middle of the night and demand: *Do you love me?* And here he was admitting it—*in absentia.* "I want to see your eyes when you say that, Reese Kreuger," she muttered aloud. Today!

In a fit of overwrought emotion she scrunched the note into a tight wad and threw it against the wall.

Damn it, Reese. I made it this far with you. How could you leave me now? To go on alone into danger? After all, we're partners in this peril. And I'm going to see it through with you!

She grabbed her ripped skirt and soot-blackened blouse. Only somebody desperate or forced into it would wear those awful clothes. Of course she always had her overalls. Actually, she reasoned, it wouldn't matter what she wore, for she had a plan. . . .

The diamond-ringed hand shook with fury. "What do you mean, they got away?"

"We're not sure how it happened, Cornell. They were in a secure place. But we're combing the city for them now."

"Get them, damn it. Both of them. There's been nothing but trouble ever since that black-haired little female appeared. Who the hell is she anyway? Stop them before they stop us!"

"Yessir. Today's the day. Guaranteed!"

"If not, Jacoby, you're a goner too!"

"It'll be today, sir. We'll get them both."

CHAPTER SEVENTEEN

"More coffee, mister?"

Reese nodded bleakly to the waitress and then hunkered over his steaming cup. Ravenously, he devoured two sweet rolls as he waited in the little coffee shop across the street from the Federal Building. He looked like the survivor of a raging fire for he wore what was left of the gray trousers and the white shirt, soot and all. Neither looked like the exquisite garment he and Tohni had purchased just yesterday. Nor did he look like the stable, well-intentioned man who'd stood, briefcase in hand, waiting for the elevator yesterday.

Today Reese didn't care about his appearance. Perhaps his disarray would serve to verify what he had to say to Mr. Michael O'Hara. If not, he could show physical bruises from yesterday's assault. Certainly the media would be interested in what he had to say even if no one else cared. Perhaps he should have thought of them first.

He was weary. All he wanted was to finish what he'd started so many months ago and return to Atlanta. And Tohni. *Tohni. Oh, how he loved her!* He hoped she'd do as he instructed in the note and go on back home. Oh, she'd be hopping mad when she realized she'd been left behind. But he simply wouldn't expose her to any more danger.

Yesterday had been a nightmare. When that hoodlum grabbed Tohni's hair and jerked her around, Reese had gone a little crazy inside. He couldn't stand to see the pained expression on her face, and he'd had to restrain himself to keep from strangling the man. He'd never had that urge, so strong and uncontrollable.

But when the leader had produced that gun, he knew they were in serious trouble, and one wrong move could've meant disaster. It had scared the hell out of him.

There'd also been the niggling fear that Tohni would do something bold and reckless, like dig for that damned gun in her purse. Thank God, she hadn't. But she had punched big Mort in the kidneys. Reese chuckled to himself and shook his head as he remembered the scene. Little Tohni reaching up to swing at that big bruiser!

Privately, Reese had been relieved when they took her purse. He didn't want her to have the opportunity to use that gun. Hell, he probably shouldn't worry about Tohni York, cool, detached agent with all her experience and training. In a pinch she usually proved to be pretty levelheaded. Which was what made her so good at her job. The job she'd given up for him.

Reese glanced at his watch, gulped his coffee, and headed across the street. He would meet Michael O'Hara first thing this morning, come hell or high water. Then it would be over. Or so he thought.

He walked steadily through the lobby, cautiously looking around, then took the stairs. He damn sure wouldn't be caught in the elevator again.

When he reached the eighth floor he paused to catch his breath. Reese checked in both directions before stepping into the hallway. It was empty except for a cleaning lady, slopping a soggy mop across the tile floor. She moved right into his path and Reese walked around her, trying to avoid the growing wet spot she was making on the floor.

Then he halted. *What's a cleaning woman doing here at this time of the morning?*

He wheeled around.

The scruffy old cleaning lady bent over her mop, slapdashing the thing in every direction. She wore a red bandanna about her head, a dowdy lime-green sweater that drooped unevenly at the bottom, a bedraggled black skirt that fell below her knees, pink knee socks, and purple tennis shoes. She looked like someone straight out of the old Carol Burnett show or . . .

"Tohn—!"

Reese didn't have a chance to finish her

name before a fist buried itself deep in his mid-section. Caught off-guard, he went down to one knee with an *Oomfff!*

The cleaning lady vaulted into action. She pressed a beeper attached at her waist inside those swaths of baggy clothing. Then she dipped her mop into a specially prepared solution of ammonia water in the bucket, and flung it into the face of Reese's assailant.

Just before contact she recognized the hoodlum. Mort!

"Aaggh!" he yelled, and reeled away, holding his eyes and screaming in pain.

Out of nowhere another man lunged at Reese. Reese threw a hard punch that met his attacker's jaw with a sharp crack. The man swayed unevenly, and the cleaning lady cleverly drove her mop handle into his belly, staggering him. He bent double, yelping in agony.

The cleaning lady gave Reese a satisfied smile and circled her thumb and forefinger to signal okay just as a bevy of building security guards and local police arrived.

"You two okay? Looks like you can handle yourselves pretty good," one of the guards commented as he reached for the first assailant.

The cleaning woman nodded succinctly. "Just take them into custody, Officer. We'll definitely file charges." She unhooked the small box at her waist. "Here's your alarm. Thanks for your help. And for staying on the alert. It happened sooner than I expected."

"Tohni."

She turned around and pulled the red bandanna off her head. "You okay, sport? For a mild-mannered, deep-thinking man, you sure get yourself into a lot of trouble."

Reese's voice was husky with emotion. "Oh, my God, Tohni, what would I do without you to rescue me? For a pip-squeak you sure pack a wallop. And you're hell with a mop."

She grinned sheepishly. "We make a pretty good team, sport. I wish you wouldn't try to keep me away from all the fun though. You know how I love the thrill of the chase. You really socked that oaf a good one there. Might have broken his jaw."

"I can only hope I returned a favor." Reese grinned wryly. "He should have to slurp noodles for six weeks. I know I should be angry at you for not doing what I told you to do, Tohni, but I'm so damned glad to see you. Where in the world did you get all this?" He motioned to the mop and the roller bucket.

She laughed. "It's a long story. The building security guards helped. Buy me a cup of coffee sometime and I'll tell you all about it."

"I'll buy you more than that. How about a new dress? One to get married in. That one is so frumpy."

"Reese—" Tears of happiness sprang to her eyes. "Say it. Say you love me as much as I love you."

"Tohni York, I love you more than I could ever say." He opened his arms and she flung

269

herself into them, laughing and crying with a renewed joy that surged all the way to her toes.

"Uh, Ms. York," the security guard said. "Excuse me, but do you know this guy?"

Tohni looked up and smiled. "Oh, yes! We're . . . we're partners. I want you to meet Reese Kreuger."

The two men shook hands.

The city policemen who had joined the building security guards were busy hauling the two huge assailants away. The guard who had worked with Tohni shuffled, embarrassed, from one foot to the other. He hadn't counted on this open display of affection between the lady and the man they were supposed to rescue. They were such a strange-looking couple too. They looked like they'd just stepped out of a wacky TV game show that required its contestants to look weird. And they certainly did.

The guard gazed curiously at Reese and handed him the abandoned briefcase. "The lady says this belongs to you. It was turned in yesterday. Someone found it in the elevator."

Gratefully, Reese clutched the handle of his briefcase. "Thank you, sir. I can't tell you how much I appreciate this. There are some valuable documents in here. If I produce a key that unlocks it, would that be proof enough that it's mine?"

"That's all right, Mr. Kreuger. We know who you are. And we take your word for it. Ms. York produced all the ID we need."

Reese looked quizzically at Tohni. "How did

270

you manage that since they took your purse yesterday? You had no ID."

"I told them this was urgent and they should call Joe. At home. He was his usual grumpy self, but he confirmed everything I told them."

"You make a great little detective, pipsqueak."

"Drop the 'little' or you're in big trouble, sport," she threatened, then turned back to the guard. "Which way to the EPA offices, sir?"

He pointed. "End of the hall, on the left."

"Thank you for all your help." She smiled and shook his hand. "Would you do me a favor, sir. Just stand here and watch us until we enter that office. It's been an extremely long and hazardous trip. And we're so close now I want to make sure we get there."

He gave her a strange look, although at this point he knew he shouldn't be surprised by anything this woman requested. "Sure. Go ahead. Glad to be able to help." He nodded.

"Ready, Mr. Kreuger?" She turned formally to Reese.

"Ready," Reese answered, and offered her his arm. They proudly traversed the last few yards of their long, perilous journey. His clothes were in sooty tatters and hers were unbelievably sloppy. But they didn't care. This was it!

"Reese, I was as mad as a wet hen when you left that note telling me to go back home. How dare you?"

"Tohni honey, I love you so much I nearly

271

went crazy when I realized you were in the same great danger as me. I didn't want that to happen again."

"You've never said you loved me until today, Reese."

"I've never loved like this before, Tohni. It took me a while to realize what I felt."

They reached the office of the district director of the EPA and disappeared inside.

The security officer picked up the mop and pushed the roller bucket down the hall, trying not to slosh the pungent ammonia water on his shoes. So far it had been a doozie of a day. And it was only nine-thirty.

Two days later, back in Atlanta, a gorilla poked its fuzzy fist at a doorbell.

When Reese answered the impatient ringing, the gorilla quipped, "Guess who's coming to dinner? And if you say 'the gorilla of my dreams,' I'm gonna bean you!"

Reese fell back, laughing, and pulled the gorilla into his apartment. He looked down the hall, then latched the door quickly. "I thought for a minute there was a gorilla at my door."

"You said to come incognito."

"Did anybody follow you?"

"Ape-solutely not!" Tohni quipped, pulling the gorilla head off. "Only the people from the zoo."

"I can't understand why. A gorilla driving a car down the street in the heart of Atlanta shouldn't attract too much attention."

"Actually there is a suspicious character outside your apartment."

"What do you mean?" Reese stepped to the window and peered through the blinds. "Are you talking about the guy in the brown Mazda across the street? He's okay. He's my official watchdog."

"Official, huh? Sounds like things haven't cooled down at all. What's going on?"

Reese waved his hand casually. "Ah, nothing. The federal guys got all excited and sent someone over. You know how they are."

"You must be pretty important if they want to protect you."

"I've been trying to tell you that all along. I keep getting into trouble and they just want to make sure I don't do that anymore. So I'm a prisoner in my own place."

"And I'm here for a conjugal visit?" She raised her eyebrows. "So how about a kiss?"

"I've always wanted to kiss a gorilla." He pulled her against him and pressed his lips to hers in a long, loving kiss that left no doubt about his feelings for her. "Hmm, I've missed you."

"You just left my apartment yesterday."

"Last night was miserable without you."

"Reese, is there still danger from Ansel? I thought your reports had him wrapped up."

Reese smiled grimly. "Oh, he's wrapped up all right. He's been subpoenaed to appear in court and a court order has been issued to halt all dumping by the company. Plus a class action suit for damages has been filed against Ansel Chemical Corporation. So if they're still functioning, it's at a minimum. Unfortunately, Ansel carries a grudge and has all sorts of hired services at his disposal."

"Like more goons he can hire to find you?" Tohni frowned. "Oh, God, Reese. Then Joe was right that night he warned us you would be a marked man?"

Reese smoothed her forehead with warm, strong fingers. "Now don't get yourself worked up over this. They'll take care of me. That's part of the bargain."

"What bargain?"

"I'll tell you later. Right now I'd like to strike a bargain with you." He kissed her again until she began to squirm.

"I hate to break this up, but I'm burning up in this fur suit. It's getting very heated in here. I think I'd better take it off."

"Does that mean I have to let you go?"

"It would be difficult to accomplish with your arms still around me. But I'm willing to try. I always loved a challenge."

"Let me. I always loved undressing you," he murmured sensuously, and turned her around to lower the zipper. His hands slipped inside the suit to encircle her waist from behind, then moved up to cup her breasts.

"Reese! The suit! Pu-leez!"

"Oh, yes." He eased it from her shoulders and smiled devilishly. "I can't resist one more joke. Do you know where they raise baby gorillas?"

She pursed her lips and thought for a minute. "In gorilla beds?"

He pushed the costume down past her hips, caressing all along the way. "On monkey ranches."

"I should have known you'd come up with some cornball gorilla jokes!" She giggled and stepped out of the hairy legs of the costume. She wore cool green shorts and a bright yellow T-shirt.

"Why, Tohni darling, it's really you under all that fur. And nice and warm too." He ran his hands along her smooth bare legs.

She gave him a genuinely happy smile. "You've talked so much about that gorilla suit, I thought you'd like to see it in action."

"The gorilla suit is great, but I'd rather see you in action," he murmured, and pulled her against him again. "With me."

"Later," she mumbled between kisses. "First I want a tour of the place. Do you realize I've never seen your apartment? We have to determine if I'll fit in here. Or if we should move into my place when we get married. Plus you promised dinner, remember?"

"A tour? Okay. All halls lead to the bedroom. I'll be glad to show the way. This is the living room."

She gave an approving nod at the sleek modern furniture gathered around a low teak coffee table. "I see you have conventional furniture, like sofas and chairs."

"That's what usually goes in a living room."

"Usually, but not always." She followed him to the hall. "We won't have any trouble fitting my stuff in here."

Reese led the way through the apartment. "We'll see the kitchen later because that's where the food is. This is my office."

"Wow!" Tohni exclaimed as she walked into the room. The place was lined with bookshelves actually filled with hundreds of books. Hardbound, official-looking books, not knick-knacks and souvenirs interspersed with paperbacks. A well-organized desk, a computer, and two large filing cabinets completed the room. "It's a real office, Reese. And to think I crammed you into my sewing room. This place is designed for real work."

He shrugged. "That's what I usually call what I do."

She sighed. "I don't know what we'll do with all my sewing stuff. It'll never fit in here. Maybe somewhere else?"

He gave her a pained look, but didn't comment. Instead he tugged at her arm. "And this is the bedroom. Would you like to see what kind of work I do in here?"

"Ohmigod! This place is gorgeous, Reese! What a bed!" She waltzed into the room, gray eyes large and full of glee. "I've never slept in a waterbed before, Reese. And it's so big."

"It's king-size."

"It's absolutely beautiful. Fit for a king." The bed extended from wall to wall and was covered with an exquisite silvery-satin spread that made the whole thing even more appealing.

"And his queen. Are you sure you don't want to skip dinner and . . ."

"You promised to fix dinner for me tonight," she insisted. "Anyway, I want to know about that important call you got yesterday from Mike O'Hara. And why you rushed away so fast."

"Later," he promised. "Let's eat first. Have a seat in the living room. I'll bring it in there."

Reese joined her with a tray loaded with food. One by one he placed the items on the table. First came a bucket of fried chicken. "The Colonel's best. Pickled pigs' feet, an old southern favorite. Hot pickled okra. Marinated artichoke hearts. And sour-cream–flavored potato chips!"

Tohni laughed with delight and framed his face with her hands. "You old sentimental sweetheart. That's why I love you so much. This is my very favorite meal. And my favorite way to eat it. With you."

"Ah, Tohni," he murmured between kisses. "I love you because I never know when to expect a gorilla at my door. You keep me laughing. And loving."

"You're such a good cook, Reese."

"Ditto, pip-squeak."

"Wonder if we can hire Stella to cook for us

after we get married. Surely Mama and Joe can spare her one or two days a week."

"What? Have Vera Lee and Joe actually decided to tie the knot?"

Tohni shrugged and shook her head. "Well, they're talking about getting married. It's amazing. I think they're head over heels in love, Reese."

"What's wrong with that? It can happen to anyone. Look at us." He opened the jar of artichokes and offered her one.

Tohni popped one into her mouth. "My mother has always looked at marriage as a business deal. And she's done quite well for herself. But this time, well, I think she's serious about loving Joe. And I know he's crazy over her. That's what she talked to you about that day in the park, isn't it?"

Reese took a chicken leg and crunched it between his teeth. "Yep. She wanted to know if I thought it was unwise, at her age, to yield to the temptation."

"My mother said that?" Tohni stared, aghast. "And what did you tell her?"

"I told her to listen to her heart," Reese said, smiling.

"How sweet," Tohni said softly. "Oh, Reese, you're terrific. And I love you so."

"I also told her that all the money in the world wasn't worth a damn when there's no love between a man and woman. She listened." He motioned to his own chest. "Voice of experience."

"Oh, yeah? Well, it took you long enough to realize it."

"And I wasted a lot of time too. Maybe Vera Lee and Joe won't waste so much time, and get right down to the loving."

"Reese, you're wonderful. . . ."

When they'd finished eating, Reese nibbled at her ear. "Do you know where a hundred-pound gorilla would sleep around here?"

"It had better be in your waterbed!" She laughed, clinging to his broad shoulders.

He swung her up in his arms and headed for the bedroom. "No more delays!"

"This is what it's going to be like forever, Reese. I love you so. . . ."

They made love. Wildly. Passionately. Sweetly. But when Tohni tried to talk about the commitment they had both made, that of marriage, Reese clammed up. Finally she said, "What's wrong, Reese? Don't you want to get married?"

"It's not a matter of what I want." He paused with a heavy sigh. He'd put off telling her long enough. He had to tell her. "I can't. Not now anyway."

"You've changed your mind about us?"

"Tohni, it has nothing to do with the way we feel about us. It's more than that. You see, I've been summoned to testify before a Senate committee this week on illegal toxic-waste dumping. There will be a major investigation of illegal dump sites all over the country. The information will come from people who know

279

first hand of midnight dumping. People like me, who have knowledge about violations and have documented evidence, are key witnesses."

"Reese, that's wonderful. This is what you've been working for all these months."

"Yes. Now, at last, the information will be made public. And something will be done about the transgressors. I'm pleased with the action the Senate is taking. Also, they've formed a task force to handle health problems related to hazardous waste in the environment. Things are finally coming together on this problem."

"So, what does that have to do with us?"

He paused, and then his voice was tight. "After I testify I'll have to go undercover for a while, until this mess with Ansel cools down. Right now things are pretty hot. That's why they sent a watchdog to keep an eye on me. They want to make sure I show up at that hearing."

"When is the hearing?"

"The latter part of this week."

"Reese darling, if you must go undercover I'll go with you."

"Tohni." He drew her to him. "Tohni darling, you can't. It'll be too dangerous for you. I will not expose you any more than I already have. Anyway, I'm not sure where I'll be going. They're taking care of my flight to Washington. And then I don't know."

"I don't care where we go, Reese. I want to be with you. Always."

"Tohni, I love you. And I don't want you to be in danger with me."

"Haven't you learned by now, Reese Kreuger, that we're in this together? Partners, no matter what."

"Not for this, Tohni. I just can't do this to you. When things calm down, I'll be back. I may have to change my name—"

"For how long?" Her tension was evident in the sharp tone of her voice.

"Maybe a year. Or two."

"You're leaving me for a year or two? Reese, I couldn't bear that! I can't believe you'd agree to such a thing!"

"Tohni, I have no choice. I'm a marked man already because of my case against Ansel. I'm not safe even now. So I may as well make it good and tell all I know. It's something I must do. Believe me, I spent some agonizing hours deciding this. It was not easy. And yet I really don't have any choice. Things will never be the same for me because of Ansel. I'll never be completely free."

"I want to go with you. I'm afraid if you go I'll lose you. What if this drags on and you never come back? Or what if they—someone—finds you? Or what if . . ."

"Tohni, please. Don't do this to yourself. You won't lose me. I'm yours. I'm sure we can make some arrangement for you to come visit. When I get settled. I'll talk to Senator Blake about it.

You could travel incognito and no one would ever know."

"Senator Hobart Blake?"

"Yes. From Tennessee."

"What does he have to do with this?"

"He's conducting the hearing. I met him that night I spoke at the Catfish King. Remember I went out afterward to talk to some of the legislators? Well, Blake was there. Something I said must have hit home."

"Everything you said that night hit home. And Senator Blake has always been a champion of the people. Uh, so they say." Tohni smiled. In the pitch darkness her gray eyes glowed with hope. A plan was beginning to form in her devious little mind. But would it work?

Reese reached out to her in the dark. "Tohni . . . I love you so much. Please believe me when I say I don't want to leave you for one minute. But I can't risk your life anymore. I couldn't live with myself if anything happened to you." His lips molded to the shape of hers, his tongue teasing them open. He tasted sweet and minty, and she wanted to press him to every part of her.

"I'm a big girl, Reese. I can take care of myself." Her tongue met his, teasing temptingly. "I love you too, Reese. And I never want anything to come between us." She pressed her small, warm body to his and yielded to his pleasure and forgot about her plan . . . temporarily.

CHAPTER EIGHTEEN

The subcommittee room was hot and crowded. TV cameras and lights were clustered in front, along with committee members and key witnesses.

From her spot in the back of the room Tohni couldn't see Reese. Actually, if she'd been in the front row she couldn't have seen him because of the crowd. It was just as well, for she certainly didn't want him to see her. Not yet anyway. She had a wonderful surprise for him but didn't want to distract him now from the business at hand. Nothing should interfere with that.

She could hear his testimony. He'd been talking and answering questions for more than two hours. His voice, once dynamic and strong, was now growing hoarse. She knew he must be exhausted. Soon it would be over. Then they could be on their way.

To her, he sounded wonderful. Tohni's heart swelled with pride as Reese related what he knew about Ansel Chemical Corporation and how he'd fought a losing battle against a company that didn't give a damn if its practices were hazardous to the public. Her heart ached when he told of the assaults and the kidnapping designed to keep him quiet. As his testimony started winding down, an aide of the Senator's approached Tohni.

"Ready to go, Ms. York? We'll let Mr. Kreuger wait in a back room until the crowd moves out. He can make the changes there and we'll exit by a rear door."

"Fine." Tohni followed the aide through the crowd. She stood alone, waiting in the back room for Reese. Waiting for her life to change more drastically than she'd ever imagined it could. Waiting for a new life with Reese.

She could hear an increase in the decibel level of the crowd. He must be through, she thought. She caught fragments of shouted questions obviously directed at Reese.

"Over here, sir!"

"Did you file charges against Ansel?"

"How do you feel about—"

"I'll buy your exclusive story for—"

"Aren't you Reese Kreuger, former son-in-law to Ansel?"

The door burst open and suddenly he was there. Facing her. She was expectant. He was puzzled. Then they were in each other's arms, baring their souls, healing their wounds, pledging their love.

"I'm so proud of you, Reese. You've risked everything for this."

"I've ruined our lives because of it, Tohni. But I had to do it."

"Nothing's ruined, darling."

"Tohni, Tohni . . . I love you so. . . ." He hugged her tight and buried his face in her neck. "I didn't know you were going to be here. I have to leave right away."

"Yes, we do. So you'd better hurry and change."

Reese raised his head and pushed her to arm's length. His blue eyes searched her face. "We? Tohni, what are you up to?" He looked down then and noticed her clothes, or rather her costume.

His eyes traveled from her white blouse with perky plaid scarf to her short tartan plaid skirt and then down to her red knee socks and black loafers. Then he looked again into her dancing gray eyes. "Tohni, what the—"

"We're going to Scotland, can't you tell? We both have jobs there. You'll be monitoring offshore oil drilling for safety. I'll work with the government helping people adjust to immunity programs just like this one. My district will include England, Scotland, Wales, Ireland, and Scandinavia. So change your clothes. We have a plane to catch." She shoved a shirt box into his hands. "Put these on."

"Tohni, I thought you understood I wouldn't put you in any kind of danger." His mouth was a grim, determined line.

"It's all been worked out, Mr. MacTavish." She smiled devilishly. "You and your wife, if you ever have a wife, will be working for the government in Scotland for as long as it's necessary. Or as long as you want." She took his hand and squeezed it. "Oh, Reese, don't you understand? We'll leave this room as two different people. No one can trace us. And the government will provide protection. It won't be dangerous. However, driving to the airport will be extremely hazardous if you don't hurry." She pushed him into the small adjoining bathroom.

"Tohni." He spoke through the closed door. "Tohni, I don't know about this."

"Don't worry, Reese honey. Great-uncle Hobart and I have it all worked out."

"What?" He poked his head out the door. "Great-uncle who?"

"Well, you see, Senator Hobart Blake of Tennessee is Mama's distant cousin on her father's side," Tohni explained. "The last time he saw me I was four. But he remembers me and certainly remembers Mama. They're what we call kissing cousins. Anyway, he helped me arrange everything."

Reese stepped out. "You always did like to take things into your own hands. I shouldn't be surprised at anything you arrange. God, Tohni, I do love you."

"But, Reese honey, you aren't ready." She looked at him, dismayed.

He glared at her. "I refuse to wear a skirt."

"It's called a kilt. The men in Scotland wear them all the time. And they're very masculine."

"Not me." Reese smoothed his thickly padded red-and-green-plaid vest. "This will be quite enough, thank you."

She smiled and stood on her toes to kiss him. "Your nose is a little crooked now, but your legs are still a perfect ten. Why don't you show them off by wearing the kilt? And those great green knee socks!"

He gave her a withering look. "Sorry, darling, you'll be the only one to know what's perfect and what's not."

"Hmm, sounds like a good deal to me. You look very nice with red hair, Mr. MacTavish. And that beard looks almost real." She grinned and patted his vest. "Been putting away too much shortbread though."

"Aye, I'm hoping my future wife learns to cook soon because I don't think the Colonel has any shops in Scotland."

"Don't worry. We can live on love."

"Didn't your mama ever tell you the way to a man's heart is through his stomach?"

"She said, 'Whenever you go fishing, be ready to net a big one.' And I've got me the very best."

"Well, you've netted me, and outfitted me. I love you, Tohni York. I can't wait until I can change your name to Kreuger."

"It'll be MacTavish, Reese honey." Tohni kissed him again and pulled a perky red tam over her dark curls. They hooked arms and walked out into a new life, partners forever.

The perfect gift to give yourself __and__ someone you love—

Motherhood: The Second Oldest Profession

by ERMA BOMBECK

"The biggest on-the-job training program ever," is Erma Bombeck's description of motherhood, that ageless institution filled with all *kinds* of moms: the one who writes Christmas newsletters that rhyme; the mother who eats her children's Halloween candy after telling them the ants got it; and the shameless ones who have discovered that guilt works wonders in motivating kids.

Erma is a thing of beauty (thighs *don't* count) and a joy forever. MOTHERHOOD is her treasure trove of love and laughter, fun and old fashioned wisdom. Buy a copy for yourself and one for someone you love. You'll *both* laugh out loud!

15900-8-18 $3.95

At your local bookstore or use this handy coupon for ordering:

DELL READERS SERVICE—DEPT. B963A
P.O. BOX 1000, PINE BROOK, N.J. 07058

Please send me the above title(s). I am enclosing $_____ (please add 75¢ per copy to cover postage and handling.) Send check or money order—no cash or CODs. Please allow 3-4 weeks for shipment.

Ms./Mrs./Mr._____

Address_____

City/State_____ Zip_____